King of Jerusalem

Hans Georg Jakobowicz

ISBN 13: 9780692025406

ISBN 10: 0692025405

Chapter One

Beach

Moist sand underfoot and the feel of saltwater streaming between the toes: such simple summer pleasures aren't spoiled by knowing that a crowded city waits just around the shoreline's bend. He was walking along a New York City beach that seemed empty on this weekday when, straight ahead, sometimes in and sometimes out of the water, a body stretched itself into the surf. It was a muscular, male body yet one that looked boyish, supple, as the breaking and retreating of the waves massaged the torso and limbs. The bather had thrown his head back and turned his face away, so a cheek, an ear, and a mop of curls were in the walker's line of sight but not the frontal features. Behind the bather, up on the sand and safe from the lapping tide, were clothes heaped in a small pile and a blanket smoothly spread out. The walker headed toward them, went past them, and stopped about a cross street's width away. He dropped the bag he had been carrying but didn't open it. Without removing either his shirt or jeans, he sat down on the sand, crossed his legs, and looked out to sea. It was a clear day even far offshore, with the horizon appearing as a distinct band, darker than the water or the sky.

After a while, the bather stood up, went out into deeper water to rinse off, turned around, and headed for the spread blanket and pile of clothes. He could have been a Phidias figure, the sculptor's Hermes, born from the sea, for there was a spring in his step and great ease even after noticing that he was no longer alone. He wore no bathing suit. Pulling a comb from under the pile, he passed it quickly through his curls, put it down, and with a smile called hello to the seated figure. The smile and the greeting having been returned, he invited the new arrival to join him on the blanket.

"You know, this is officially a nude beach now, so if you want to swim, just take your clothes off. One has to be careful, though, not to touch anything excitable even by chance because the police scour the beach with binoculars." He had a slight British accent, his curls were mostly blond with a few darker strands, and his penis was ample, displaying a foreskin as snug as a snail's shell.

"No, thank you, I don't want to go swimming right now, but I'm enjoying talking and looking. How long have you been in America?"

"Did my accent give me away, or my foreskin? I came here for college and finished that two years ago. When I phone home, they tell me I sound Yankee now, but I guess not to a true one."

"I'm not from here either. I left my birthplace quite young, but New York is home now. I'd miss it if I had to move. Where else could you bathe nude on a nearly tropical beach and be just a stone's throw away from utter urbanity?"

"Don't you miss your birthplace?"

"I don't know. It has changed so. It changed even the few years I lived there. So many people are gone. It was Vienna where I was born. That place has many pasts."

"Did you leave voluntarily? You seem too young to have had to flee the Nazis."

And without waiting for a reply the bather asked, or rather wondered out loud, "Perchance are you a Jew?"

"Like you, I'm not circumcised. My life, though, would have been quite different if I'd remained in Vienna." And then they said nothing for a while. Both were on the blanket now, the newcomer again sitting cross-legged and the bather reclining comfortably. They looked at each other, examined one aspect or another, gazed up and down the beach and out to the horizon and then again at each other. A wind sprang up, a cool one, and the bather reached for the pile of clothes and pulled on his shirt. He didn't dress further right away but then, after more minutes of silent thoughts and probing looks, said that he would have to head back into town. They left the beach together.

Chapter Two

Walls and Views

It was more than a mere stone's throw to either's apartment, and much of the way they had in common. Waiting for the bus, they talked; they talked on the bus and then on the subway. They told each other routine things about their New York lives. As their paths were about to split, the bather suggested they both go to his place. The answer he received was neither a yes nor a no.

"At 8, I'm due crosstown and can't invite you along because it's to a performance that's sold out. I have to be there. My not going is out of the question, not the least reason being that I know some of those involved, and also the piece is about my birthplace, Vienna. Still, if you let me shower at your place, I'll be able to make it and not look like a total vagabond."

At the bather's apartment, they showered together and then, wrapped in towels, toured the rooms. It was a large place, six floors up, with outside walls mostly of glass. The views it gave were of the East River and of glass walls in a perpendicular part of the building. Also, tucked into the building's corner, one saw a single, old brownstone five stories tall—apparently the lone survivor of what once had been a tenement row.

The rooms of the bather's "flat"' were suitably furnished for so much glass. The manner was deco and must have cost much. Oddly, nothing hung on the flat's painted walls—not a single picture, mirror, or clock. Although the walls' colors were lush—the fresh green of an Alpine meadow in the dining room, the glow of golden oranges in the kitchen, blue inclining to a lavender sunset in the guest room—the absence of any objects on them startled the visitor. In the bedroom, there was a tall bed, high off the floor with three tall posts that dominated the space. It stood like an altar pointing up to a ceiling pure blue as a cloudless Adriatic sky. The bed was unmade. They lay down on it, untied their towels, hugged, kissed, and proceeded to finger each other's foreskins.

"Haven't seen many of these since I left school in England," said the bather.

"I was too young in Vienna to play with such toys," the guest replied. "Guess I was a late starter, all of 15, and it was at a beach almost as empty as ours was today."

"I hope you had no watchers. If I could have been sure we had none today, I'd have ripped your clothes off as soon as you sat down on my blanket."

Their fingerings intensified, and given their courtship of several hours, they climaxed without delay. The visitor needed another shower, and when he emerged from the bathroom, his host was standing naked in front of the bedroom's window wall and appeared to be gazing into the top floor of the old brownstone. His body was astir, stretching and relaxing gently, as if it were still being massaged by the surf at the beach. Was he displaying himself for someone in the other building who was looking but couldn't be seen?

"What are you doing?" the visitor asked.

"Teasing. I have a curious neighbor. You'd better get going, though, or you'll be late for that performance."

The visitor took a clean shirt, a carefully folded jacket, and a dressy tie from his beach bag, unfolded the jacket, put on the fresh items, and was ready—with his close crew cut and the sharp contrast between the semiformal blazer jacket-dress shirt-neckwear combination and the jeans and sneakers—to attend a premiere. After all, this was the casual summer season. Before leaving the apartment, he and his host exchanged names and phone numbers. The host's name was Herbert Phanariot, and the visitor's name was Joshua Haburghe.

"Is that a Viennese name, Haburghe?" asked Herby. Josh's reply was a noncommittal shrug.

Chapter Three

At the Theater

So sold out was the theater on June 23, 1977, that the downstairs lobby had become an obstacle course for those who had tickets waiting. Seekers of spare seats pestered everyone in the will-call line for the chance no-show. Joshua picked up his single ticket, a complimentary one. He was puzzled that the seat next to his remained empty during the first portion of what was a triple bill at the ballet. The new work, the one about Vienna, was the evening's midpiece, and just as the lights began to dim for it, a man came to occupy the empty place. His appearance was severe, not just because of his suit's cut and how he held himself but due to his sharp features. As the music began, he didn't relax but instead seemed to be forcing himself to sit still. Only when there were people to see on stage did he stop broadcasting his unease. There was plenty to see.

Scene 1: Sunlight slanting down through a décor of leafy trees dapples the stage floor. Suddenly, from behind the tall trunks of brown bark, figures appear. They come together, forming a handsome assembly. The ladies are in light summer gowns, and the men in dress parade uniforms. Stepping lively, they begin to waltz, their dancing shaping itself like a game of hide-and-seek in this romantic out-of-doors. One couple in particular catches the eye. She, although flattered by her companion's gallantry, tries to elude him, relentlessly. Her rapid skips and runs are declarations of independence, flights of freedom, launchings for liberty until—until she pauses, confronted by his demeanor's gravity. She seems to take note of what he is wearing—black and gold, the House of Habsburg's colors. This isn't just another young officer. Could it be His Majesty? She curtsies deeply, slowly, and on the ascent expects to be bid adieu. He, however, remains. Taking her hand, he helps her to rise and engages her arm. Together, thoughtfully, they step forward, out of the woods.

Scene 2: In a clearing, in the moonlight, elfin beings emerge. From out of the shadows, they take to the air. Compared to the forest's daylight denizens, these are virtuosi of the waltz, the fleeting Fanny Elsslers of this stage with their partners—fauns and satyrs in disguise. Nights are short in the springtime of the year, and its spirits need to make haste before speeding away, before vanishing as the sky brightens, the woodland warms, and human steps are heard approaching—those of a boisterous crowd, intent on pleasure, a little forgetful of propriety. These mortals have vigor, but what might be their course if not controlled? Is there a suggestion of vehemence, a hint of violence? For now, though, these plebeians dance lustily to sate their safer appetites for drink, touch, and loud laughter.

Scene 3: Indoors, amid upholstery—red velvet, black satin, silver fringe—a multitude of lamps emits a precarious light. This is the realm of the demimonde—courtesans accompanied by rich cavaliers, impoverished nobles rescued by wealthy widows, and, like spice, a sprinkling of artists. Love here is slanted, twisted, fluted, and more than a little cruel. Stances are convoluted, yet bodies still sway in three-quarter time. Can such couples live together happily ever after? Let tonight stand, and in the morning, coffee and *Kipfel* suffice.

After that, who knows? Arrangements such as these seem utterly urbane, consummately civilized.

Scene 4: Silvery shadows sway on mirrored walls as a young woman—solitary, wrapped in her isolation as if wearing a cloak—glides through the dynastic twilight into a courtly ballroom and commences a stately waltz. She steps one, two, and curtsies, three, to no one visible. Perhaps her deep reverence is to a dear memory. She steps again, resplendent in her refinement, resigned to the emptiness that surrounds her. Suddenly she is dancing with someone. He carries himself proudly; his concern for her is calming; they are about to sweep cobwebs away and stir up a breeze—it has the hint of mint, like dawn's gust moving the bedchamber's gauze curtains to prompt one last embrace. As suddenly as he appears, he is gone. Her turning slows, its pulse grows faint, her steps echo like a lone bugle's midnight plaint. She is in mourning, her myriad reflections fragment, her replicates implode, and yet, where just a moment ago she had danced alone, the world and all her pasts assemble, chandeliers blaze as if volcanic, the music's lilt is waltz and dirge conjoined, and the pleasure of uncounted pairs of dancers peaks. The stage is one vast vortex now. A nation's tragedy entertains history's audience.

Applause for the new ballet lasted and lasted, curtain call followed curtain call, but finally as Joshua and the latecomer could step out of their row for the intermission, both were moved to comment on what they had just seen. "Too many stereotypes," said the latecomer.

"Archetypes, perhaps, but don't they suit that music?" responded Joshua, modifying the statement he would have made into a reply. He wanted to continue the brief exchange but had to respond to a hello and, meanwhile, lost sight of his critical seat neighbor in the crush of the foyer. Perhaps their conversation could continue at the post-premiere party Joshua had been invited to attend. However, his neighbor did not return to his seat for the program's final work.

Chapter Four

Party

They didn't see each other right away. The theater's atrium was becoming crowded, the ballet company being a confluence for several of New York's social streams. Joshua, after entering, went to fetch himself a glass of wine and then began waiting patiently to pay his respects to the ballet's makers. He was standing alone, at some distance from the circle surrounding the ballet's choreographer, a man still dapper and boyishly edgy although aging, and its instigator, the ballet company's director, a big man who bounced mischievously from pose to pose. Taking a sip of the beverage he had been poured, aptly it was Green Vetliner, Joshua was startled by a sharp voice from over his left shoulder. "You liked the music?" he was asked.

Turning to face his erstwhile seat neighbor, Joshua countered, "What was there to dislike? All the pieces were fine, popular fare, appropriate for the topic."

Came the parry, "Too dancey, too much the same, all um-pa-pa."

Joshua frowned, "I heard something else. To me, Johann Strauss's beat and cadences establish the base line, the healthy norm. His music's spontaneity and mobility felt comfortable right away. Lehar's way was already a little distorted and with a retard, whereas Richard Strauss's waltzing seems self-consciously simple on the surface but underneath is sensually, sadly complex."

"The whole construct is too clever by half. I'll bet it wasn't the choreographer's doing. It seems a rabbinical contraption."

At that moment the circle around the choreographer and instigator opened, and these two men, who were still without drinks, nodded to those they were leaving behind and started walking to the bar, past Joshua and the man whose contraption comment had raised both of Josh's eyebrows. Pausing, seemingly in recognition, in front of this pair of party guests, the ballet's makers nodded hello, but before either guest could say anything, the choreographer, looking at Joshua, asked, "Was the waltzing Viennese enough for you?"

Josh replied, "More than that, every scene was right for its milieu and time. Congratulations!"

The choreographer just smiled, but the instigator, addressing the severe man, declared, "Too waltzy for you, I'm sure, but you can't be bothered with appearances; your dances don't acknowledge the benefits of masks and disguise." Then the choreographer and the instigator, both again giving nods, continued on their way to the bar. Joshua turned to his erstwhile seat neighbor and asked, "You choreograph?"

Assenting dismissively, the man wondered, "And you are a waltz expert?"

"I can do the steps, but for the life of me, I can't dance. In between steps, I stumble when I ought to glide; I freeze up instead of flow, yet I love nothing better than to look at dancing when it is done well."

"Ah, an impotent expert! How fitting for this claptrap. I don't doubt that you dare to write about dance. You must be one of the notorious New York critics."

"I did translate some historical notes about waltzing for the program booklet. That's why I was at the premiere and am at the party. I don't recognize you, although I thought I knew most choreographers working in New York."

"I've not been here in a long time, not since my student days. Switzerland is where I'm based, the German part."

"Ah, I ought to take this opportunity to practice my German. I read it a lot, but it isn't the same as speaking. The conversational language keeps changing constantly, and I find mine becoming somewhat dated."

"A dose of old-fashioned German would be good medicine for the homesickness I've felt the last few days, after being here for a month. I don't recall craving for the cradle when I was in America before as a student. Of course, I'm more set in my ways now. Still, perhaps we can do the German some other time. English is this party's currency. I'll pronounce my name, though, *auf Deutsch*. I am Heinz Burckhardt." His was a definite "u" in the Burckhardt and not an "e" as in Berkshires. He appeared to be in his 30s, at most 40, somewhat older than Joshua, so might have been born before the start of World War II. Joshua then introduced himself.

"Haburghe doesn't sound *Deutsch*," was Burckhardt's response, "so your speaking German isn't for family reasons, at least not for paternal family ties?" Joshua didn't answer the question, and his silence might have become awkward if they hadn't been interrupted by an elderly pair, a refined and frail gentleman, whose clothing looked a little shopworn, and a regal, richly dressed woman with a crown of silver hair. The gentleman exclaimed to his lady that here was the person to answer her question about the new ballet's title, whether the German *Wiener Walzer* should be translated as a singular or plural.

"The original Viennese ballet of that name, Louis Frappart's, involved several different waltzes, just like tonight's New York derivation, but, you are quite correct, the German title by itself could be either one or many." Joshua, knowing both the gentleman and the lady, proceeded to make introductions. "Allow me—Countess Zdenka Podhalka, Edwin Denby, and Heinz Burckhardt. The countess was a futurist dancer in her Paris past, Mr. Denby is our finest dance writer, and Mr. Burckhardt, whom I've just met, is a choreographer from Switzerland." Looking at Burckhardt, Josh continued, "What sort of choreographer, if I may ask, ballet or modern?"

"A good one, if I do say so myself. In Europe these days, we don't anymore distinguish between classical and other. We fuse. It is called contemporary."

"Just as inept a term as "modern dance," exclaimed Denby. "Our choreographer tonight uses movement from the streets, from the stables, and from the popular dance floors, but he has the knack of making it look classical when he combines it with ballet."

"He can't help himself!" Burckhardt uttered in his most clipped way.

"He can't help his response to the music," Denby countered. "He worships music, good music, and would never bring himself to violate its nature."

"Movement has its own logic, and the choreographer's task is to see it through whatever in music or design it chances to encounter."

"Illogic is often what gives dance its reason to be, what endows it with charm. Your dances must be earnest indeed if you choreograph as you criticize."

"Back in the days of the first "Vienna Waltzes" being too serious in ballet wouldn't have been tolerated. The emperor himself would have forbidden it," interjected the countess. "Franz Josef took a personal interest in what was, after all, his company of dancers. That was why even an August Bournonville couldn't establish himself in Vienna. The emperor preferred Paul Taglioni's ballets. Franz Josef neglected none of his privileges and titles, and there were odd ones among them. He was, for instance, not just sovereign over Austria, Hungary, Bohemia, Slovakia, and other pieces of European sod, but somehow he had also inherited such titles as Emperor of Mexico and King of Jerusalem. It must have been from the Habsburgs' Holy Roman Empire legacy, going back to the time of the Crusades, from which the Jerusalem title stems."

Burckhardt hadn't been paying attention to the countess. Women didn't count much in his estimate of things, but what she had said now mattered to him. "Is that still a valid title?" he wondered.

"For some people, yes, it is!" replied the countess. "The ultra-Orthodox Jews in Jerusalem don't recognize Israel's government because there can be no Jewish state until the advent of the Messiah. They certainly don't want to be governed by Palestinians. So they have petitioned the United Nations to send them the current heir to the Austrian-Hungarian throne, Otto von Habsburg, as their ruler. Amusing, no, if that would solve the Jerusalem dilemma? However, no one so far has told the petitioners yes or no." With that said, the countess asked Burckhardt where she might be able to see some of his dances. "And, to accompany them, have you any use for my poor Czech composers? Everyone neglects them so."

She appealed to him as if Smetana, Dvorak, Suk, Janacek, Martinu, et al. were stray puppies.

"It isn't often that I build dances to music. Thinking the dances, I never do. If music intervenes, I want to let it happen catch as catch can."

"You remind me of Mary Wigman. She had percussion as accompaniment, but really it was only to cover up noise—the panting of her dancers, the creaking of the floor. My dear Czech, Rosalia Chladek, was more honest in that respect. If Rosalia didn't want a music, she would see to it that silence reigned. She waxed the floor boards, padded the stage, and forbade her dancers even to perspire."

"No, my dances don't look like those of the old expressionist ladies. Excuse me for calling them that, but I met them only when they were aged and repeating themselves and were quite rigid in their ways."

"Well, what does it look like, your choreography?" Denby asked.

"Come to a run-through," suggested Burckhardt "May I ask Joshua here to contact you? Josh, let's exchange phone numbers!"

Joshua, a conscientious writer, always had paper and pen on hand. The exchange having been accomplished and goodbyes having been said, they dispersed into the hum of the reception, which was becoming a party, a true one when the ballet's dancers, having showered and dressed, infiltrated the assembly of guests. In twos or threes, seldom solo, these godlings engaged the mere mortals. It was part of their job, and they knew how to start a conversation, how to stop it neatly and move on to the next knot of patrons. After the first few of these divertissements, the dancers would interrupt their routine. Because habitually they ate little all day until after the performance, they regrouped at the buffet tables. Substantial food had been prepared by a Viennese chef's team. For those wanting a full supper, there were small schnitzels in a delicate batter and two salads—a potato salad with what the Europeans mean by mayonnaise and a cucumber salad in an apple cider vinaigrette slightly sweetened with honey and spiced with dill. For those wanting a snack, there was an array of sliced sausages, cubed cheeses, diced radish, dark bread, and creamy butter. For desert, there were mini versions of tortes—Panama, Hapsburg, Wind, and, of course, Sacher. Most of the dancers selected the bigger meal, talked among themselves between mouthfuls, and then resumed their mingling with the guests. The wine having flowed liberally by then, people from both sides of the footlights showed their true interests: the ones who wanted to talk aesthetics and those who wanted to gossip and, naturally, those looking for pickups both straight and gay. Also, among the dancers, those ambitious to choreograph had antennae out for patrons.

Joshua, given his afternoon caper, was curious about who at this party, other than dance people, he knew. He set out to circulate. The first familiar face was Jocelyn Ady's well- preserved one. An international show girl, she had married rich and, after her husband died, knew how to hold on to his money and her looks. She joked about long gone days and nights in which she danced the cha-cha and the Charleston at Las Vegas and Paris clubs but had always gone to see the ballet every chance she could. "So in my decrepitude, I've decided to support it. Believe me, those ball gowns for the last scene cost a lot! By the bye, I liked your passing allusion to the Nazis!" she said in referring to Joshua's program note. "Did you get to see any of the rehearsals?"

"No, I had my first glimpse of the ballet tonight," he replied as she had already begun to move on. The next moment, there was tiny, fiery Dr. McCannery with a lady on his arm. Was she one of his patients? He liked to escort his particularly interesting female cases around town. This one towered over the good doctor but seemed shy. Josh had been treated by McCannery after picking up a parasite on a trip to translate for a conference in the tropics.

Also circulating by himself was Paul Smyth, a big-boned lawyer who advised foundations and trusts. He was going from group to group and getting into too many of the photos being snapped by the party's pair of paparazzi. One was Adelaide de la Salle, a socialite who had craved a career and turned herself into a competent portrait photographer. The other was Mr. C, a scholar specializing in ancient physics, whose dance photographs were becoming collector's items. Josh knew them both and had no difficulty eluding their flashes. Eventually, he found himself encountering the same people over again. Also, the number of dancers at the party had decreased, and so he decided to go home and get some sleep.

Chapter Five

Loft

Heinz telephoned Joshua to relay particulars of the run-through to which he had invited him, Denby, and the countess. It would be the following week, but he suggested that the two of them meet sooner—to which Josh wasn't averse. Although sometimes thoughtful and contemplative, Joshua hadn't yet a set constitution. Being an optimist at this time in his life, he believed that "a lay a day" was healthy. He had found Heinz attractive and off-putting at once: The man's firm lines appealed to him. The brusque manner, although he wasn't even a Berliner, was a barrier that begged to be breached.

Josh was certain that Heinz found him desirable, so he suggested they meet for a supper. A restaurant would be neutral ground and yet could serve as launching pad for what might follow.

The supper was on the Upper East Side at a new Hungarian café Josh had heard about. The place's air conditioning didn't suffice for what was a hot evening, too hot for goulash, so they just ordered chilled sour cherry soup and, for desert, Joshua a slice of Dobostorte and Heinz a serving of apricot strudel. Heinz was still finishing his glass of Neusiedler Weissburgunder and Josh, who had emptied his, called for a few cubic centimeters of Strohwein to accompany his piece of pastry, his *etwas suesses*. Their conversation seesawed back and forth, English or German alternately cresting. Heinz wanted to know about Josh's work. "I like language, spoken and written, and have a job as translator at the United Nations. The UN job pays most of my bills. I also write because I want to. Mostly it is about the arts. That's how I became involved with the ballet project."

"Did you study at a German university?"

"No. My college and graduate studies as such have been in America, but I had translator training at a *Gewerbschule* in Vienna. And you, where were you trained and what about your American stint?"

"Folkwang, in the ever-so-romantic rust of the Ruhr Valley. But post-World War II, it wasn't all Kurt Jooss and *Ausdruckstanz* if ever it had been; it was very mixed. There was even some genuine blood-sweat-and-beauty ballet of the Russian sort, not just the regimented German type. My sojourn in America was in a suburb of Chicago with Sybil Shearer. It was intense. During breaks, she made me go to try classes in New York, at Connecticut College, and even in California. So I got to see the country as well as the dancescape."

They were lingering over a few sweet crumbs on their otherwise emptied plates and looking at amber droplets clinging to the clear glass tumblers that had held wine. It was time to go. Desire and curiosity had mounted mutually. It was Heinz who said that they ought to head to where he was staying. "I'm subletting a loft. It isn't far from here. The owner is on sabbatical. It's a five-floor walk-up. Hope you don't mind climbing."

They took the Second Avenue bus down into the upper forties, got off, turned left toward the East River, and stopped walking in front of a brownstone that Joshua too recognized. It was the lone tenement that stood nestled in the embrace of a glass-walled apartment building's two wings—the one he had been invited to after being at the beach and before attending the ballet. He said nothing to Heinz as they entered the stair hall and walked up past several apartments per floor to the top landing. Heinz took out his keys, undid a pair of locks on this level's only door, opened it, and flicked a wall switch, turning on the lights. A large, almost empty space appeared. They entered, and Heinz closed the door. The walls of the loft were painted white and hadn't a blemish despite the lights being bright, stage lights. A wooden dance bar was affixed to one long wall and ran nearly the length of it, cutting across the lower fourth of several windows that were fitted with straw draw blinds. A shorter, free-standing bar in the middle of the floor was supported by metal legs. The opposite wall was a mirror image except that no bar was affixed to the length of it.

In Josh's expectation, this wall ought to have had actual mirrors between its windows, but there were none.

Heinz began to draw up the blinds and open the windows, a much-needed action in the absence of air conditioning. He went about it ceremoniously, and it took time, for there were a goodly number of windows. The room's floor was wood of a pastel color. Heinz had taken his shoes off and so did Joshua, this being a dance studio. The floor boards seemed sprung as Josh walked over them in his stocking feet. Heinz led the way to curtains at the far end of the floor. He drew them aside to open a long alcove. It was bedroom, bathroom, toilet, kitchen, clothes closet, storage space, study—all in one except for bookshelf separations. The whiff of being neat and clean more than of being lived in and cramped issued from it. Josh was invited to take a seat, either on the single chair or on the bed. He chose the bed. Heinz sat down next to him. They were turned toward each other and took hold of each other's shoulders. They kissed. It was a long kiss during which Heinz's lips remained drawn and dry but Josh's became pliant. As their heads and holds separated, they reached for each other's crotch. Both had erections. Heinz began to undress Josh, who reciprocated. They had to stand up to finish removing their last items of clothing, and then they paused, facing and appraising one another. Heinz was the taller of the two and had an athlete's sinewy anatomy. Josh's lines were soft and pliant on his moderate frame. "You're an admirable average from a casting director's point of view!" said Heinz.

"What role do you have in mind for me?" quipped Joshua with a laugh.

"Would you mind if we acted out a scene, something I fantasize about but hope won't turn you off?"

Josh gestured "What?" to Heinz, who went to the alcove's storage area and pulled out a pedestal on wheels. A pair of tall military boots, shiny black leather ones with metal buckles, were affixed to the top of the base. The boots swayed slightly as Heinz pulled the assemblage across the floor. He also brought out a military cap and swagger stick. On the cap were Nazi insignia—an eagle and a swastika.

"Please put on the cap and stand in those boots!"

"You want me to play the part of a SS officer? Me? It's you who are the tall, blond Nordic type."

"Please!" said Heinz, as if it weren't a request but a command.

"I've had to play quite a few roles in my life, so what the hell!" Josh, holding the cap he had been handed, mounted the pedestal and inserted first his left leg and then the right into the boots. He had lost his erection, but he put on the cap at a rakish angle and pulled up his chest and straightened his back to pose there in a military manner, holding the swagger stick against his left side. He was slightly alarmed but couldn't deny also experiencing a thrill. Heinz stared at him. A sliver of a smile in Heinz's features let Josh know that he was doing well in the part. Heinz bent down over Josh's penis, took it between his lips and began to suckle. As Josh's erection returned, Heinz shifted from an awkwardly bent stance to a more comfortable crouch, his knees resting on the pedestal's front edge as if in a pew. Heinz knew how to elicit pleasure. Having established a rhythm with his head action, he used his left hand to fondle Josh's testicles and also began to masturbate himself with his right hand. In due course, Josh climaxed. Heinz swallowed, which seemed to trigger his own ejaculation. A torrential load spilled from his hand onto the floor. Immediately, he went to fetch towels. Josh was still standing in the boots when Heinz had finished wiping off their flesh and the floor. "Climb out of those things," he said to Josh. "Come rest on the bed. We really should talk." Silently, but with utter civility, Heinz opened his refrigerator and offered Joshua something to drink. He poured them each a glass of white grape juice and, after placing the bottle back into the cold, joined Josh on the bed.

Outside, light still lingered in the sky, the tardy and wistful illumination of an evening in early summer. A window in the glass building opposite lit up to show a male figure standing nude, swaying seductively and staring straight ahead towards them. Heinz got up from the bed to lower the nearest window shade and commented that he had acquired a tease.

There are few restrictions to post-coital conversations. Topics range from the personal to the political. Only previous experiences of the erotic sort are unlikely to crop up. "There's something I've been meaning to ask you," Josh began when Heinz had returned to the bed from lowering the shade. "What did you mean by the remark about the waltz ballet being rabbinical?" Josh was in an inquisitive frame of mind.

Heinz was in a mellow mood. He sighed. "Let me try to explain. Our world, our civilization, our society is built on traditions. Of course, traditions, customs, communal habits can evolve, improve, and even perfect themselves. They can also be degraded. Alien ideas, foreign feelings, corruptions can corrode them. That is what I see happening. Shrewd intellectualizing is swamping true sentiments. The whole idea of that ballet is a sham. It purports to show the fate of an entire empire, of a fine people—both rulers and those ruled—by way of the history of waltzing. It proposes that a healthy, vigorous way of life must inevitably decay. How clever yet how untrue! The waltz may have become decadent and died, and, yes, the Habsburgs have been discarded, but something of that empire's way of life persists. Habits of thought and behavior the Habsburgs fostered, in fact, inculcated in the population, remain. That dynasty prepared the way for Hitler and his acceptance by the people. Of course, Hitler made mistakes. He was utterly right, though, that the people wanted cohesiveness, solidarity and not debate, faith and not doubt, and that is still so today. Who conceived that ballet? I don't think it was the choreographer. It is an example of subversive thinking, which especially the Jews have been at ever since they infiltrated into Europe. They question our heritage and negate it.

"You mean that the ballet company's director, a Jew, devised a scenario to show how dilapidated Christian Europe had become? That he deliberately maligns the West? That he is part of a vengeful plot going back to the Jewish diaspora? That's quite a conspiracy theory you have! You can't be serious. That fits neither history as I've learned it nor the man; I know him."

"I keep making the same mistake, jumping too quickly from the particular to the general and back again. The situation is complex, like a tapestry, and my arguments ought to be woven with as much patience and detail. The state of ballet is just a small part of what's happening. It involves all the arts, even the sciences and, of course, politics. Look at the

Near East. So much sympathy for the illegal state of Israel, no sympathy for the Palestinians!"

"Yes, that's quite a leap from a waltz ballet to the Wailing Wall. I could give you a counter-argument, the Jews not as corrupters but as people who have kept the Western world alert, on its toes. That line of thinking, though, is equally wrong if it assumes intent."

"Oh, my accusation isn't about something necessarily conscious; it needn't be a plot, a vendetta deliberately handed down from generation to generation. Indeed, it is most likely subconscious, a temperament that's inherited and therefore all the more insidious."

"How many Jews do you know? Coming from *Mittle Europa* in post-Hitler times, I'd guess not many. Having grown up here, I know quite a few. They are as varied and adaptable as any other racial group."

"Do you deny the differences between beagles and pincers?"

"I've encountered cuddly poodles and vicious ones. Humans are extremely educatable. We can learn to be good and bad. Whatever our inherited mood swings, we can adapt them, modulate them. For survival, there has to be emotional and intellectual variety within any family whether it is a Nordic, African, Jewish, or Palestinian one. I'm going to see to it that you meet some Jews here in New York."

"You're the teacher type, I now realize. But no, no thank you. The passing acquaintance I've had with a few, like the director of the ballet company, is lesson enough. I don't want to get closer!"

"You have been closer."

"What do you mean?"

"You've just had supper, sex, and an argument with a Jew."

Heinz blanched. His forehead grew moist. A fury stared from each of his eyes. Both he and Joshua were still naked, the night being hot. Heinz rose stiffly from the bed and went over to the place on the pristine floor where Joshua had put his clothes, picked them up, walked to the loft's door, opened it, added Josh's shoes to the pile, went to the landing, and hurled all his guest's belongings down the stairwell. The only thing he said was "Uncircumcised Jew!" but he held the door open to evict Joshua.

Joshua stared back at Heinz saying nothing. The thought that kept recurring to him was how queerly life imitates art: here he was a nude descending a staircase. He hoped no one else would use the stair hall before he had reached bottom, put his clothes on, and walked out onto the street.

Chapter Six

The Showing

Plans for Josh to bring Denby and the countess to Heinz's loft for the dance showing had been made prior to Josh's naked expulsion from the place. Heinz added additional people to his guest list but was unsure what Josh would do—attend, not attend, or might he even tell his friends that the run-through was canceled. Heinz had to know for sure. He decided to phone Josh not to apologize but to explain that they would have to meet again for propriety's sake—that decorum must be maintained in public. When Josh heard Heinz's voice, he hung up on him and did so again on Heinz's further attempt to find out. However, Heinz had been right: Josh was a teacher—by temperament, by choice, and because it fueled his curiosity. Besides feeling that he owed it to Denby and the countess to keep the promise of accompanying them, he resolved to be utterly formal with Heinz. If he maintained his composure, perhaps it would show that bigot that this Jew at least knew how to behave.

The climb up the stairs winded the countess. Denby, used to his own stairs in Chelsea, took the ascent in stride. When the door to Heinz's loft opened, it wasn't he who asked them to enter and take their shoes off. Herby Phanariot stood there invitingly. He introduced himself to Denby and the countess as a neighbor of Heinz's and to Josh said, "We've met before," flashing a broad smile to accompany this matter-of-fact phrase. Herby led them to a cluster of folding chairs set up to face the curtained far end of the loft. People—five, to be exact, two women and three men— were already seated, and Herby saw to it that everyone introduced himself or herself. Apparently, no one else was expected and although the loft was fairly bright with daylight, Herby threw the switch for the overhead theater illumination and then took one of the two chairs that had remained empty for himself.

Heinz appeared from behind the curtains, dressed in his work clothes—white T-shirt, loose black slacks, dance slippers—and welcomed his guests to show them what he'd been working on since his arrival in New York a month ago. Then he called out for the dancers to please make their entrance. As they stepped out from behind the curtain, one by one, Heinz pronounced their names. There were seven, four men and three women, dressed alike in pristine practice clothes—white tops, white tights. They spread out along the long bar, spacing themselves evenly. Heinz seated himself in the last empty chair, twisting sideways in order to see the dancers. Apparently, he preferred this less comfortable position to turning his chair to face the sidewall. His guests followed his example.

To begin with, the dancers stretched and bent, extending their limbs and lifting their torsos, then folding or flexing at the joints. What they did resembled a routine dance warm-up initially. It was balletic—pulled up, turned out, held in—but not strictly. Ease of movement was not its only goal, for at times there was visible pressure, stress, strain, thrust. Elegant motion and emphatic movement alternated for a while but then began to combine, so what the dancers did started to look like choreography and not just training.

At this point, the seven left the bar and reassembled in the middle of the floor, in front of the curtains. Here they could step more spaciously and have more room to jump and turn. Moreover, the audience was able to face forward and feel less constrained. Characteristics of class work rather than dancing still clung to the action, even when individual members of the cast paired. Now couples could swing and engage in additional partnering holds. Heinz had gotten up from his chair for these passages and joined the demonstration so that the number of dancers would be even. Only when he seated himself again did it seem that actual dancing had been attained. It started in silence and was intensely patterned: a cluster of three dancers counterpointing a cluster of the other four; then one versus one versus five; then three pairs plus a single. Some of the performing units did extended adagio, others lively allegro. It seemed inventive but came to a halt when Heinz turned on a tape recorder near his chair. The dancers, grouped, were poised to listen but didn't immediately respond. That moment made them seem one with the audience. Their breathing diminished so that the loft was silent except for distant street sounds coming through the open windows and the faint snake-like hiss of the metallic tape in the recorder. The first musical sound was that of a piano—chords and then ascending notes. Two wind instruments joined in. A rhythm grew, more implied than established. It was three-quarter time although the downbeat kept changing place from measure to measure. Four dancers now began to waltz, the three women and one of the men. Pretending to wear voluminous gowns, they used one hand to hold up the imagined skirt, swinging it back and forth, while the body turned, dipped, leaned, and spiraled. The other arm they held around emptiness, as if space were a partner.

The three men not waltzing stepped high in a complex parade rhythm, a *défilé* such as one might see the Lipizzaner stallions do at the Spanish Riding School. In the music, Joshua thought he recognized the Zarathustra waltz from Richard Strauss's *Thus Spake Zarathustra,* but it had been reconfigured as a trio in the lean manner of late Stravinsky.

If the waltzing hadn't "the unbearable lightness of being" in which ultimate waltzing partakes, Josh nevertheless had to admit the ingenuity with which it and the marching were juxtaposed. Then came two simultaneous solos, one a woman's and the other a man's. Much of the woman's motion was down on the floor, *Tieftanz,* in this instance impulse and involuntary action being as crucial as what she did deliberately. She took positions a sleeping body might twist itself into and corrected them. She assumed poses that a listener seated a long, long time might be entrapped in and eased out of them. When she placed herself carefully and properly, the surge of maintaining equilibrium, volume, form could be sensed in her being. At the end of her solo, she walked off seeming happy to leave her battlefield behind. The man's solo, upright, was a set of abstractions on mimetic themes. What began with facial expression and gestures migrated into the torso and leg musculature. Both dancers' execution was clear, the woman being crystalline to the point of bravura and the man forging his flesh into steel. No music came from the recorder during the double solo, yet the pulse of the soloists' breathing seemed part of a purposeful soundscape, something planned. The five other dancers had gone to the side and leaned silently against the bar watching the soloists. On occasion, they shifted their stances, one or two of them reflecting the "on-stage" action, but the audience could see that only by looking to the side. There was music again for the finale.

No question but that Josh was intrigued by what he had watched. Heinz might be a bigot, but he definitely was a talent. So had been one of Josh's favorite composers, Richard Wagner. Josh's resolve to be an iceberg in Heinz's presence was thawing. There was applause for the dancers in which Josh participated. When Heinz took a solo bow, Josh did not clap with his hands but nodded approval.

The assembly, both audience and performers, dissolved into clusters. Josh turned to one of the dancers whom he knew from social encounters and a pleasant sexual one. Denby went to speak with Heinz, and the countess with a dancer who had a Czech surname. When the cast disappeared behind the curtains to change, it was time to depart. Heinz stood at the loft's door to bid each of his guests an individual goodbye. Came Josh's turn, Heinz simply said, "We must talk," and Josh replied, "Yes."

Chapter Seven

Over Coffee

The countess called Josh. He had to come to *Jause*! Well, urgent was what she would relay; the small repast she was preparing was merely scrumptious. She had no money to her name worth mentioning yet knew how to live well. She did things for people, and they became obliged to her. In her ministrations, she didn't discriminate. Both the high and mighty and those unlikely to fall because of their low perch benefited. On this visit to New York, a lovely penthouse apartment had been put at her disposal, and as she bid Josh to enter, she gave her guest the feeling that this was her own domain. It was half past four on a summer day, and here above the city, with the doors to the terrace standing open, the air was fresh and breezy. The countess wasted no time on pleasantries or rehashing Heinz's showing. She led Josh to a small table with two minimal settings, a coffee pot, a bowl with whipped cream, and a tray of small sandwiches that looked as if it had been flown in from Tresniewski's Vienna buffet. Instead of a sugar bowl, an unopened jar of clover honey formed a triad with the pot and bowl. Sitting at this table afforded a fabulous view of the city, but the countess didn't give Josh the chance for that.

"I've heard from your family," she said as she began to pour coffee.

"Which family?" was Josh's response.

"Don't play games. There's no one left except for you on your mother's side, although I have news, good news I think, about restituting the Heine holdings."

"That can wait; it has waited a long time as far as I'm concerned."

"Long ago for you, but to me your mother still seems actual. The way she tossed her head when she spoke! Her hair would settle back ever so neatly. It was bobbed and brown like chestnuts and looked lustrous when she was well."

"What does my father's family need from me? Get on with it, please!" Josh was being abrupt even though remaining frugally polite. "I'm certain they want something."

"My dear, the Habsburgs have learned not to want. They have, though, made a request. His Highness has a task for you, something that can be executed only by someone directly in the family line."

"You say 'executed'. It sounds unpleasant. And, conveniently, I'm now, all of a sudden, in the direct line of descent?"

"Evidence of a legal, binding marriage between your parents has turned up. It was during the war and at a place far away from their familiar surroundings. Circumstances were such that records had to be hidden and documents disguised. Your parents, who were rather young, married in Salonika, which had recently been occupied by Hitler's forces. Your father, although a Habsburg, hadn't been spared from being drafted into the German military and was there as an occupier. Your mother was a refugee from Germany, having been sent there presumably for safety by her Jewish family. Salonika had a branch of the Heine bank with a loyal staff. The two young people had met socially before the war. He recognized her during a round-up of Jews in Salonika and helped her to escape. It necessitated his desertion."

Joshua, about to say something, didn't but nodded for the countess to continue.

"The two young people lived and fought with the Greek guerillas in the mountains near Salonika. Quite a few of those bands, which included both Christian Orthodox Greeks and Greek Jews, eluded the Germans throughout the war. The family has at last located individuals who not only knew your parents but where documents were kept. It seems your parents were married, married twice—once by a rabbi and once by a priest."

"That would require a double divorce to rend asunder!" Josh tried to joke as he sat straighter in his chair.

"Don't be flippant. Listen. What happened then and there has shaped your life." The countess was becoming impatient with someone she cared for. "Later, your father was with a small raiding party captured and executed by the Germans. Your mother was already carrying you and continued to live among the guerillas. Your birth, under rudimentary conditions, weakened her. She returned to Germany after the war only to find herself alone. Most of the Heines had died or been killed. A few of them had fled but were far away and out of contact. For a short time, your mother seemed to be regaining her health. She fought the loneliness. That's when I met her. Soon, though, her strength gave out again. She died in the bad flu of 1947. Knowing your father's family, I was able to hand you over to them. They accepted the responsibility but, supposing you were illegitimate, had you brought up out of sight, at that boarding school here in America, the one you fume about."

Joshua's annoyance had dissipated. The countess could see that he was sitting almost resignedly in his chair. She continued with her mission as envoy from the Habsburg dynasty to its prodigal son. "His Highness wants to see you; I don't know what about. When can you come to Europe to meet with him and be officially welcomed into the family?"

It was summertime, and Joshua's vacation was coming up towards the end of the General Assembly's long break. He had a month and left it to the countess to negotiate the exact spot, date, and duration of his courtesy call on the former rulers over Austria-Hungary and accreted soil.

Chapter Eight

Honorary Aryan

Herby Phanariot arranged for Heinz and Josh to meet again, but wasn't himself present—not even at the window opposite. He must have been out and about. In Heinz's loft, there were just the two of them. The situation was tense in terms of soul and sex, so they started by talking about Heinz's dance. "There was much I admired." Josh confessed.

"What not?"

"That you didn't use the full scope of technique—no pointe work, no demarcation of the five-foot positions or total turn-out, not high enough a carriage or sufficient ease of articulation at the joints."

"Dancers of the Kirov Ballet haven't been put at my disposal. Besides, in addition to generalized ballet, I use techniques not taught in ballet class."

"No objection to that as long as they are consonant with the classical base, but I find that the lack of toe, leg beats, brush steps, and emphatic placement deprives contemporary dance of a richness it could have."

"To make those devices, your hallmarks of genuine ballet, appear anything but studied, to transform them into spontaneous expression is impossible. Not even your *Vienna Waltzes* choreographer succeeds in doing so. Too much pattern, too much musical form act to abstract his feelings."

"I'm sorry you feel that way about form. I find true form, significant form, a manifestation of feeling."

"How rabbinical of you!"

"What the hell have you against the Jews?"

"Just that. They dispute but can't intuit. Form isn't feeling. According to the Bible, the world was without form when the spirit of God moved and began to create. Form came later; it followed the urge to do, to make."

"Who now is being rabbinical or, as I'd call it, Jesuit?" Josh had been standing, and Heinz, after opening more windows and readjusting the shades, had sat down on his bed.

Josh was close enough that Heinz reached out and pulled him onto the bed. They did not kiss. Instead, each gazed at the other's face, and after some time, they began to undress one another. Still, they delayed. Josh stared at Heinz's chest with its taut nipples, and Heinz at the supple motion of Josh's rib cage. Finally, they lowered their eyes to look at the other's penis. This time Heinz involved none of his props, nor did he bow down before Josh. The sex was angry, grab bag—hand action, skin contact. They fell asleep after finishing. When they awoke, the loft was dark and through the windows they could see that a light had been turned on in Herby's apartment.

"No use my pretending that I don't enjoy you, Jew boy." Heinz said more to himself than to Josh. "Even in Hitler's innermost circle, there were those who couldn't do without their honorary Aryans."

"I don't feel honored; in fact, I'm horrified. Yet I'm here because I need to know; I have to understand. How can you hate so systematically, so abstractly? To hate those who have harmed you is, well, natural. But to hate a people just because they aren't your own clan is madness in the modern world."

"Not because they aren't my own. I haven't anything against Tibetans or American Indians, but Jews are perversely intertwined with the Germanic people."

"Is it Christianity that you hold against the Jews, that the gospels of a Hebrew, Jesus Christ, were imposed on your forbearers? I admit, Christianity has its distasteful doctrines—celibacy instead of sexuality, humility instead of natural pride, disdain for material reality. Christianity did, though, civilize Western society, at least for a while."

"You are right about me. I do not care for Christ. He corrupted the idea of a direct, singular God. I don't believe in salvation, only in evolution. May the fittest men survive and perfect themselves and their offspring in his image."

"Just as there is no such thing as an abstract ballet, there is no such thing as an abstract god. Your god, as you allude to him, is conceived in the image of man even though an ideal one. Those you say are evolving toward him are supermen. And if you believe in superior men and a god man, you also must believe in inferior humans. Am I to be your pet, your subhuman plaything? You are today, I hope, really unique in your beliefs."

"Not at all. In fact, I want you to come to a meeting. You'll recognize some of those attending. They were at my showing too."

"Is Herby part of the group?"

"He's looked in on it, but is far too pagan to join. He's not aware of the difference between us and Jews."

Chapter Nine

The Conspirators

It was a small group that gathered one evening after supper in an apartment on the Upper East Side. Heinz's instructions to Josh had been precise. The building at 413 E. 90th Street was named "Linus," and he was to press button 5E at the entrance. After being buzzed in, he would have to walk up to the fifth floor and stop at the first right-hand door. Heinz met him there and ushered him into the apartment's living room. Josh recognized several people who had been at the dance showing but couldn't remember their names. Tonight, introductions were by first name only. The apartment belonged to a man and woman, a couple he hadn't met before. Passing the mailboxes downstairs, he had looked at the name plates and seen Hoffmann on 5E. As the Hoffmanns, Alex and Zara, explained in the casual conversation preceding the meeting, theirs was an heirloom place. It was rent controlled and had been passed on to them by the man's parents, who used to live there when the neighborhood, Yorkville, had been German—*echt Deutsch* because Christian Germans had settled there, whereas the city's German Jews had congregated on the Lower East Side and later on the Upper West Side. Some of Yorkville's restaurants, taverns, and delis still dealt in German fare. Josh learned that his host was an engineer and his hostess a painter who taught art in a private high school. The others too seemed engaged, middle-class inhabitants of Manhattan. Heinz was the only one who spoke English with a foreign accent. He and one of the women from the showing spelled each other at being leader. Heinz explained Josh's presence as tentative—he had been recruited as a candidate to fill the group's need for a writer. "He has a lot to learn yet about politics, but when he does, perhaps he'll not disagree with us." Heinz said nothing about Josh having Jewish blood coursing through his veins and gushing into the unkosher erections beneath his conspicuous foreskin.

Initially, the meeting conversation revolved around Egyptian recognition of Israel and the caustic effect it would have on the Palestinian cause. "More acceptance by Americans of the Jewish state as if it were a just, a legitimate entity," remarked Heinz.

Having been introduced as naive, Josh felt no compunction about asking why Israel was being designated as illegitimate. His question prompted laughter, and Heinz explained. "People of Arab descent have lived there for thousands of years; theirs has been a continuous presence. For the Jews to claim it as a homeland and national state after all that time away is, we believe, an injustice to its true native population."

Josh said, "I'm amused by your concern. Everyone in this room tonight seems to be of European stock. Are you not being just as unjust? You are making your homes on land that in the past belonged to the American Indian. Isn't that what ought to worry you?"

"We can't right all past wrongs," snapped Zara in response. "What is happening in Palestine is current. It could be stopped right now. America's blind support of Israel has to be opposed. She continued less testily with, "Palestinians, whose families can trace their residence in Jerusalem back centuries prior to Zionism, are being evicted. Their houses are being demolished to make way for new habitats in which immigrant Jews will live. Just think about it, and you'll be as upset as we have become."

Josh's curiosity, not just about Heinz but about these other people, was mounting. He wanted to get to know them, perhaps even understand them. Did they really care about the Palestinians and believe that of all the world's problems theirs was foremost? Or were they just antisemites? Since childhood, Josh had been puzzled by people who saw him as a Mischling. He didn't feel mixed, split, but thought of himself as whole. He couldn't comprehend those who insisted on dissecting him and hating or loving one half but not the other. The group of people he was facing now would not, he suspected, accept him, believe him, if he gave in to their stance too readily, and so he raised another objection. "Are there not Jews in Jerusalem and elsewhere in Palestine or Israel as rooted as any Arab? The historic diaspora of the Jews in Roman times was far from total. Pockets of them remained, and immediately afterwards, expelled Jews started to return. Religious Jews have the wish of being buried in Jerusalem. They would work hard and save in their exile in order to retire to Jerusalem so they could live their last days there, be sure to die there, and be laid to rest in sacred soil. They would bring with them their entire families and households—people who seldom returned to Europe after the *pater familias* had passed away. Heinz, wasn't it one of your classic German authors, Wilhelm Hauff, who wrote stories about these people? No, Jerusalem and what lies adjacent to it was never *Judenfrei*."

Heinz countered, "Prior to Zionism, the Jews in Palestine were insignificant in number compared to its Arab population."

Josh wanted to say that returning Jews had been excluded from census taking. He also had the urge to ask whether homeland rights depended on numbers, on who was breeding at a faster pace. Instead, he commented, "Nationhood will soon be outdated anyway."

"You do have lots to learn," concluded Zara Hoffmann.

Chapter Ten

Under Open Sky

The sun crossed the sky in naked splendor almost daily that summer. Small white cumuli and cirri sometimes splattered sections of the blue expanse overhead, but cloud banks or thunderheads were rare, appearing only at night and would be long gone before dawn. It was ideal beach weather in New York. The time for Josh's vacation hadn't yet come, but with the General Assembly in recess, it was slow season at the UN. Josh went to the office early and left early in order to go to the beach. If he hadn't quite finished his assignments by noon, he'd return to the office late in the day. Otherwise, he stayed on at the beach into early evening. Usually, he was by himself, Herby and he having telephoned about going together yet somehow never did. The book he immersed himself in during the long travel back and forth between Manhattan and the beach was Adalbert Stifter's *Late Summer*. He was seeing Heinz a lot at night and on weekends. The choreographer had an allergy to sunlight and refused to join Josh's daytime outings. He was not, though, averse on an evening to sitting in the sand or wandering along open stretches of the outer harbor's much indented coastline. It was on such occasions, gazing at the darkening Atlantic, that this pair had their least constrained conversations.

"You came to dance fairly late, well along in your teens. What was your boyhood like before that?" Josh asked Heinz.

"It was spent in a seminary, one belonging to Roman Catholic Church."

"I had no idea you wanted to be a priest."

"No, it had nothing to do with my wants. I was bullied into it. Family. Once I was in the institution, the pressure continued, mostly from teachers, who all wore the collar, but from a few of the older seminarians too. When puberty hit me and my classmates, we experienced what amounted to mental castration. We were taught to despise our bodies. But mine remained real to me; it seemed God-given. I saw our teachers enjoying our suffering, and I recognized it as sadistic compensation for what had been perpetrated on them when they were young. I was walking about, sitting at my studies, kneeling in confession, prostrating myself in prayer, lying sleepless on my cot with erections. They gave me a quantum of pleasure along with the feeling that there must be something more. I had no idea how to release the pressure that kept building up within me. One day, my confessor said that if I hadn't discovered how to escape this curse, perhaps physical castration would cure my almost perpetual boner. I hadn't the presence of mind to realize he was being sardonic and alluding to masturbation; really I didn't know what it was. I had vaguely heard of the *castrati* and was afraid the priests would have me operated on. So I simply left, walked out into the town, which we were allowed to do on Sunday afternoons, and didn't come back. I had enough money on me to buy a train ticket to the nearest city. Having read about the bohemians and the hippies, who were just emerging, I headed for their hangouts. An older guy, he was all of twenty-three, picked me up, and that night I had my first sex in his mouth. Only later did I learn how to masturbate."

"Didn't the seminary and your family send the police after you?"

"I was seventeen, and there were lots of strays at the time. Right after I'd reached my majority, I wrote to tell them that I was alive and enjoying sex but gave no return address. By then, I had come to believe in the possibility that the best of mankind is evolving toward a godhead, and also I was deep into dance."

It was on such an evening at the shore that Heinz asked Josh about his religious training as a boy.

"I was an orphan. My father had died before I was born, and my mother while I was still quite small. She had no family. My father's kin, unsure of my legitimacy, hid me away in an American boarding school. Thanks to one of my teachers, I grew up a skeptic about religion. If there were such a thing as God, wouldn't the knowledge be inherent in us? I can find no notion of God, no concept whatever of such an entity, within me. It is an alien idea. Of course, you can also say that I ought to reject evolution and relativity because I'd never have discovered them by looking inside myself. Such ideas, such theorems, though, aren't the same at all. I do find the things they are based on within me, and when shown how (assuming I could manage the math for relativity) I can follow logically the necessity of postulating their existence as explanatory principles. Postulating the being of God explains nothing. Therefore, God does not exist. I'm an old-fashioned atheist."

"What do your paternal relations think about that? Are they religious Jews or freethinkers?"

"It was my mother who was the Jew. My father's family is Catholic, and they are as uninterested in and as ignorant about my beliefs as about my sex life."

"Well, you're not a Jew then. It is paternal lineage that determines one's religious legacy."

"Not according to Hebraic law. One is a Jew if born to a Jewish mother— another nice conflict like the controversy about the evening hours." Heinz looked puzzled. "Am I a Saturday or a Sunday child? I was born after the sun had set on a Jewish Sabbath, a time the rabbis count as belonging to the next day but which is still Saturday according to the priests."

Did such storytelling fortify relations between Joshua and Heinz? Facts that came to light did factor into their relationship. That Josh's paternal family was Catholic somewhat salved Heinz's conscience about being involved with a Jew. Joshua had no illusions about the disparity between his sexual attraction to Heinz and his distaste for Heinz's ideas about God, humans—ordinary ones, supermen, and subhumans. Moreover, the young translator was trying to accept himself as he was. Perhaps he even realized that chalking up his contact with Heinz and Heinz's group to satisfying a nagging curiosity—the urge to know the truth—was something of an excuse. But there were precedents for his behavior—he had read Klaus Mann's farewell to his beautiful young Nazi storm trooper. Wasn't he being as nobly conflicted in his dealings with Heinz?

Chapter Eleven

An Invitation

The Hoffmanns were having supper in their fifth-floor walk-up apartment. When by themselves, they ate at one of their two kitchen tables—the round one next to the apartment's rear window with its unobstructed view to the north. They could look up the East River to Riker's Island and to the bridges—the Triboro and that of the Long Island Railroad. Heinz had asked Zara to design the cover for a pamphlet their group intended to print and distribute. Josh had been given the job of rewrite editor. "Alex," Zara asked, "have you read the edited text yet?" He shook his head no. "There's no question that Joshua knows his craft. Nothing straggles, everything is more compact. But he's also taken out feeling. The Palestinians' plight reads like a copyright complaint."

"Do you think Joshua could be against us? Might he be a spy?"

"Spy? Don't be paranoid. No, he's not against us, just not for us, not for our cause. He has nothing against the Palestinians as such. Probably he'd like to see them and Israelis embrace—especially the males. He reminds me of that other friend of Heinz's who was so insensitive to matters of race. Heinz's recruits worry me. I don't think it sets a good example to have our group get a gay reputation."

"Now who's being paranoid? That Herbert chap attended two meetings and then decided not to join. Our couple of gays, Heinz and Joshua, make us just typically New York."

"Herbert may not be a member, but he's around. I'm uncomfortable in gay company. It is like being among Jews. They're a cold lot."

The telephone in the next room rang, and Zara went to answer it. Returning to her seat at the table, she had a wry smile on her face. "Speak of the devil; that was Herbert on the phone. He is inviting us to a party for Joshua, a send-off for his trip to Europe." She reached over and placed both her hands on Alexander's face and stroked his cheeks.

"I see you'd like to party now," he said with a smile as they got up and headed for the bedroom. Without intoning a question mark, he added, "You accepted the invitation," as he began to unbutton Zara's blouse.

Chapter Twelve

Boat Ride

Where the money came from no one in Herbert Phanariot's current, recently acquired circle of acquaintances seemed to know. He lived well without having to work. His apartment looked posh, and he drove a sports car. He hardly ever mentioned having a family or a stockbroker; when pressed he mentioned his Greek ancestry, Constantinople Greeks settled in Britain. His checks drew on offshore Greek banks. On nights out when he'd pick up the bill and those with him protested, Herby's habitual comeback was "I'm on good terms with the gods. I run their errands." Zara wondered whether he might not be a drug dealer. She had noticed that his eyes would glaze over at times, take on a vacant look. They reminded her of the blind eyes in the Greek statuary that gazed not at you but through you to the beyond. Herby would come out of such spells as suddenly as he fell into them. However, he wouldn't have missed a thing in the talk that had been going on. He'd be able to quote what everyone had said verbatim. Indeed, his ability for precise recall amazed her.

For the party he was throwing, Herby had rented a boat big enough to hold anyone Joshua wanted to invite twice over. Josh wondered why Herby was making such a fuss. "It isn't a long vacation; I'll be back before you know I'm gone."

"Somehow I'd gotten the idea the UN was giving you a foreign assignment for the fall and perhaps beyond and that you'd want to say goodbye to all the people you know here. Well, it's too late to change the plans I've made." Herby showed Josh the printed invitation. "Some have already been mailed." It was in dark blue type on a card of azure and read: "You are cordially invited to bid goodbye to our friend, Joshua Haburghe, who will be leaving New York at the end of August. This adieu will take place on Saturday, August 20, 1977, beginning at 6 p.m. We will gather at the Seventy-Ninth Street Boat Basin in Riverside Park, where you and a companion of your choice should board the Ben Franklin Ferry. Please be prompt because the boat will be set to sail. Supper will be served during a cruise around much of Manhattan. The boat will dock at approximately 8 p.m. at Staten Island, where the party will continue with a performance and midnight refreshments at Villa Olympia in the Grymes Hilltop Estates. Or, if you must depart following the cruise, you will be chauffeured to the Manhattan-bound Staten Island Ferry. Those attending Act Two of the party, can avail themselves of comfortable overnight accommodations at the estate or be chauffeured to the last Manhattan-bound ferry (12:30 a.m.). Our overnight guests will be served breakfast and offered transportation from the estate to the ferry. Please RSVP for each stage of the party. Your host, Herbert Phanariot."

Herby further explained that the boat was an old-fashioned, double-deck ferry. It would remain tied up at the basin for forty minutes to await stragglers, then would head out into the Hudson, steering north toward the George Washington Bridge and the Palisades but turn east into the Harlem River, then south into the East River and navigate down to the Inner Harbor. The boat ride would almost amount to the full Circle Line sight-seeing tour with its vistas of skyscrapers, bridges, waterways, and low as well as high shorelines. Supper aboard the ferry would feature Mediterranean food. The performance would be in the big Victorian mansion of the Staten Island estate. Its hillside perch gave splendid views in all directions—toward the glowing Manhattan skyline, to the Verrazano Narrows Bridge's pearl strands of light between Staten Island and Brooklyn, across the Outer Harbor to the communities that sparkled adjacent to Sandy Hook and out into the dark ocean dotted here and there with the gliding lights of boats. There would be six performers—a string quartet and a ballet pair. There were at least thirty bedrooms with private bathrooms in the mansion or elsewhere on the estate, but communal jacuzzis and saunas were scattered throughout the estate's park. "Josh, I want it to be a party you'll remember," Herby said.

"But it sounds so grand. I'm not a celebrity" Josh protested.

"You need to be celebrated in order to become worthy of admiration. It will be a lesson for you, and besides you'll never again be as young."

The number of people who came to the party amazed Josh. Had he given Herby all those names? Some, of course, brought along dates he didn't know, but still there were many of his dance world acquaintances and friends, UN staff colleagues, literary contacts, and even pickups. Some of the guests were the first people he had gotten to know while settling in New York. Others, like those in Heinz's cell, were recent contacts. As guest of honor, Josh was perpetually surrounded. It seemed at first that he'd not have a moment free to enjoy the boat ride's views. Still, a sense of the great city through which they were passing permeated his awareness. The city's spaciousness and densities suddenly impinged upon him. Its scale, its barriers near and far, its boundaries, express lanes, traffic jams, tunnels, and scaffoldings seemed urgent. The variety of its substance (concrete, stone, steel, wood, glass) and the diversity of its natural infrastructure (waters, rock, soil, sand, vegetation, air) came to matter. Did the city sense that Joshua was being celebrated? His pulse increased and his posture became more imposing. He seemed aglow a little. Those skeptical that so plush a party was appropriate now conceded that this guest of honor might be worthy of note. His historical note for the program of the recent Viennese ballet had struck a tone that seemed to awaken echoes in the arts cave that was New York. People asked about his plans not merely for courtesy's sake. Where was he going? For how long? What assignment had he been given by the UN? Was a promotion involved? What were his personal intentions? Would he be doing any writing?

The standard reply Joshua gave was that he would spend the vacation visiting his birthplace, Salonika, and his subsequent childhood home, Vienna. He'd look up relations and old family friends. He wasn't, though, certain where he'd be stationed afterward. It might be right back in New York at the General Assembly. If not, the assignment away would be of brief duration. He wasn't planning to sublet his New York place.

Critical of the money being spent on this party when it ought to have been donated to the arts was the ex-showgirl, Jocelyn Ady. She'd not met their host and wanted Joshua to tell her all about him and then point him out or introduce her. "You'll have the chance to see him shortly," Josh replied and was glad when Dr. McCannery urgently beckoned him away. Otherwise, he might have to admit how little he knew about Herby. McCannery had around him four of the five medical interns who shared an apartment next door to Josh's. How had the good doctor detected the like-minded in this crowd? Moreover, Josh couldn't recall having given Herby their names to be put on the guest list. On this occasion, McCannery's date was a pudgy lady in her late 40s, born in Dublin and divorced from a Manhattan millionaire. She had ventured to Manaus and contracted schistosomiasis—a curiosity along that portion of the Amazon because most stretches of its Coca Cola black waters were too acidic to support the blood fluke's intermediate host—a snail. However, agricultural fertilizers applied at some of the experimental farms had raised the soil's and the nearby swamps' pH, so that accidentally introduced snails had found a niche in which to thrive. Likely what had happened was defecation: persons infected along the White Amazon had seeded the worm's eggs from their bowels into the moist loam of fertilized farms along the great stream's Rio Negro portions. Then more snails were invaded by the parasite's miracidia and developed into cercariae, which the snails shed as if they were torpedoes launched to seek and penetrate human skin. The Irish lady had gone swimming in those infested waters thinking she was perfectly safe because she immersed herself only in the rapid flow which even the piranhas avoided.

Before the good doctor had finished his story, Jocelyn Ady joined herself to Joshua again and became a listener to the tale. McCannery gave her a brief synopsis of what she'd missed and then elaborated on how he would publish a paper about this ecologic anomaly and illustrate it with microscope images of worm eggs from his date's stool. Then the two, the doctor and his patient, went to refill their drinks at the bar while Ady again remarked what a waste of resources on medical exotica when the money could have funded great art. The interns frowned at her statement.

Also not alone at the party was Paul Smyth, the foundations lawyer. He had brought two companions, one a very young Canadian choreographer, a Peter Pan type, Joshua recognized and considered able. The other was a woman, more a girl, who spoke at a fast clip and kept taking off and putting back on a pair of horn-rimmed spectacles. Dance and dance criticism were her passions, but she was also an addict of detective stories and would write about a new ballet as if it were an act of murder. She believed that her job as a critic was to discover villains. On this occasion she was proclaiming the Canadian boy's latest effort not a success because of criminal costuming, which had gotten in the way of viewers' ability to see the dancers' bodies really respond to the dialectic between the sensual choreography and the chosen music, a bit of brainy Busoni. Joshua hadn't seen the dance and imagined at first that striped jailbird attire, worn by the cast, proved to be distracting, but as it turned out, the evil lurked not in a pattern of horizontal bars but just in too much material hiding the glories of the human anatomy.

A gong sounded, the signal for supper. Joshua wanted to linger on the open rear deck, but at that moment, their host appeared. Herby had the countess and Heinz with him and was lamenting Denby's obstinate refusal to leave his summer residence in rural Maine and return to town for this party. "I'd even have sent a chariot to fetch him," he was saying. As people around them were leaving the open deck for the supper buffet inside, the paparazzi, Adelaide de la Salle, and Mr. C appeared, wanting to document the head party. Heinz arranged a *pas de quatre* grouping with Herbert, standing in the center as host, and the countess, seated in a deck chair in front of him slightly to the right of center, himself as the framing sentinel on the left, and the guest of honor, Joshua, at his host's right hand. Adelaide was shooting in color, Mr. C in black and white. They wanted variations on the initial grouping, particularly in the *port de bras* to indicate affinities among the four. By the time they were done, the first diners had emerged onto the deck. They wore woven straw baskets, shaped like oblong trays with deep sides, suspended in front of them from a strap around the neck. It gave them a pastoral look but had a practical purpose—to facilitate carrying food and drink while walking about. "What a good idea!" said more than one guest to Herby who proudly stated, "Mine." When the lead party with its photographers went in to get supper, their group split up, mingling with others.

The gong's call had catalyzed the gathering. Up to then, the guests had remained so many molecular clusters, circulating about the boat to get views or bobbing at a favorite location but only looking inquisitively at the other clusters. Aligned for the buffet, they were obliged to have contact with those they didn't know waiting ahead of them or behind in line. Connections were made, conversations emerged, the possibilities of collaborations were projected, and previously unsuspected opportunities enticed. Herbert had counted on such a reaction. His farewell affair for Joshua was turning into a true party.

In contrast to the mingling going on among many aboard, the countess and Heinz were together by themselves. Deciding to wend their trays to a dark corner of the deck, they began to discuss Joshua. "What relatives has he in Salonika and Vienna?" asked Heinz, "You seem to know him and his background well. What are they like, these people he may look up during his holiday?"

"There are none I know in Salonika. His birth there was a wartime happenstance. Both his parents were from Middle Europe, Munich and Vienna, and that was where his mother, a young and ill widow, was repatriated after the war although she had no surviving family there anymore. Josh's paternal family, though, was large and prominent throughout Germany, Austria and beyond." Countess Zdenka seemed reluctant to be specific. She avoided naming names.

"Where did the Haburghe come from, and what precisely is its ethnicity?" Heinz wondered. The lady was starting to say something about spelling changes prompted by history or outright mistakes when Herbert appeared. He hadn't a tray suspended in front of him but was holding a glass of wine in one hand. He mentioned, in case they'd not noticed, that it was of a precarious vintage, from vineyards being started in the Golan Heights. Then, in a manner that couldn't have been more matter of fact, he stated everything about Joshua that Heinz wanted to know.

"Joshua's family name is the result of elision and camouflage. His father's last name was Habsburg and his mother's was Heine—the Habsburgs of Austria-Hungary and the banking house Heines, who were the poet's kin. Joshua has had a lot to hide and, if his legitimacy is fully established, a lot to inherit—paternal titles and maternal moneys. Should there ever be an Austria-Hungary again, he would not be far in line from His Highness Otto to become emperor."

The countess was even more astonished than Heinz. Of course, she knew the facts about Joshua, but how in the world had Herbert learned so much? It wasn't like Joshua to be careless. Had romantic circumstances loosened his tongue, or did he talk in his sleep? She took off her tray and disposed of it on one of the racks intended for that purpose. About to address the two young men, she could at first only shake her head. Finally, words emerged. "Please, if you care at all for Joshua, do not discuss this with anyone now. The matter of his legitimacy has been investigated. A decision will be made at a family council soon after Joshua arrives in Europe. Much depends on the impression he makes on His Highness Otto, who hasn't seen Joshua since he was a little boy. Otto has his relatives, his advisors, his lawyers, his confessors. He'll listen to them but make up his own mind. Any rumors now, any publicity would prejudice Otto against Joshua. There's an obstacle already, and it is Joshua himself. He is reluctant to inherit a life he feels is not his. He grew up in America, much on his own. Independence means more to him than family and family duty. Yet when I've talked to him about his parents, I think I see a yearning to take his place as their son. If he is invited into the family, please give him the chance to decide. He could always decline and return to New York, resume his work as a translator, and try to be a writer. I've known him longer than has any other mortal, and wouldn't wager on what he will actually do."

Herbert wasn't as uncertain of the future. "Much depends on the role Otto would assign our friend. Josh isn't the sort to play pretender, anymore than Otto has been with his ideas of a European parliament and its presidency. If Joshua can also claim his mother's fortune, he could put real punch back into the Habsburg name."

Heinz was silenced by all he was hearing about Joshua but not to the point of refusing to think ahead. If indeed the countess had been right about one of Otto's titles being King of Jerusalem, what couldn't he and Joshua do to bring justice to the Palestinians? At minimum, he could become a thorn in the side of the Israelis.

Chapter Thirteen

Hilltop

That the great city loomed starboard, port side, and all around the vessel, that the guests from somewhat different walks of life mingled freely aboard while picking careful paths across the decks due to the meal trays protruding in front of them like broad prows, and that summer lightning tickled the distant eastern sky–was a storm approaching from the vastness of the Atlantic?–these circumstances enticed those who hadn't initially opted to partake in Act 2 of the party to change their minds. Herbert Phanariot, being a liberal host, acceded to all late requests to attend the entertainment. He was stricter about those he was allowing at the last minute to stay overnight. Youth, looks, and being single were his criteria for tardy admission to Act Three—the pajama party. He was even supplying pajamas, bathrobes, and overnight kits to those who hadn't brought any along.

In the large ballroom of Villa Olympia, a stage had been assembled. Seating extended from the ballroom through opened folding doors into the banquet hall. Tables for the post-performance repast had been arranged instead on the enclosed L-shaped veranda. The performance began soon after the last limousine from the boat had discharged its passengers. A printed program had been prepared, but as Herbert announced from the top of stairs leading up to the lip of the stage, it would be distributed only following the performance. He wanted everyone, especially the cognoscenti and critics in attendance, to listen and look with as little prejudice as possible. The members of the string quartet made their appearance from the back of the stage. There were three young men in tuxedos and a woman cellist in a voluminous black evening gown open in front, as was her whim, to expose her naked bosom. Several in the audience recognized her as Charlotte Moorman. Only a few recognized the music. It was rhythmically vibrant yet not verbose; its tonal playfulness wasn't capricious but seemed grammatical according to rules, new ones but rules nevertheless. Undoubtedly as original as anything composed in the World War II era, the piece was difficult to place for those familiar with Stravinsky, Schoenberg, Hindemith, or Bartok.

Having finished playing, the musicians rose and bowed for the applause, and then seated themselves again as a ballet pair stepped onto the stage. She wore a white tunic with pleated skirt and pointe shoes in a just-off-white tint of cherry blossom. He had on a white shirt, open at its ample collar and billowing at the sleeves, and blue tights terminating in white socks below the knee. His blue slippers bore a white triangle at the instep in order to highlight the arch of the foot. There was no need to emphasize the arch of his crotch. Balletomanes recognized the pair as Mimi Paul and John Prinz. If the music of the initial string quartet had been difficult to place, that for the dance seemed to be by the same composer. The choreography of the *pas de deux* looked more streamlined than would a late-nineteenth century, "after" Petipa duo. Art nouveau lines curved like vines within the rectilinear containment of the stage space. The woman's steps for her solo were classical although her torso movement alternated between tense contractions and sustained relaxations, a combination that contrasted vividly with the leg and footwork. Was this dancing by Gorsky in his more experimental mood? It turned out that neither the dance nor the music were of the Russian tradition of fifty years earlier but from that era in Vienna and so chosen by their host perhaps because that city was Josh's childhood home and the place where Denby had studied. The printed program with its dark blue letters on azure paper gave the composer's name as Ernst Toch and the choreographer's as Heinrich Kroeller.

Chapter Fourteen

Midnight Immersions

Winds converged from all points of the compass to play merrily atop the Staten Island hills and keep the storm clouds at bay far offshore. It was as fresh an August night as if the season had been spring. The repast Herbert served following the performance was a post script to the Mediterranean kebab supper aboard the ferry: hot bread accompanying chilled pasta salad in a yogurt-mustard-pesto sauce. Those departing for the last ferry had been dispatched, and the ones staying overnight were seeking their bedrooms or testing the waters of the heated pools strategically situated throughout the gardens. Heinz and the Hoffmanns had occupied a secluded hot tub, one so small that no one else would possibly feel welcome to join them. Although bathing suits were not obligatory, all three were modestly covered while immersed and had worn bathrobes from their rooms to their rendezvous. It was Zara Hoffmann who first mentioned Joshua.

"Tonight's guest of honor seemed more substantial to me than he has on previous occasions. I even came to believe in his writing, the way he spoke about it showed commitment and thought. There was sincerity and graciousness in the way he received people wishing him well, and he showed his gratitude to them without making a fuss. If only he cared for our cause, he might be useful given his contacts at the UN."

Heinz took charge. "Useful, yes, but not because of his UN connections. True, he seems to know his way around there, but basically he's not much more than a flunky in that bureaucracy. What I hope will suit our ends is his family in Europe. Our Joshua may be coming into his not insignificant inheritance. There is political status on his father's side, and on his mother's, there is money."

"European connections shouldn't concern us," Zara objected. "Most of the EEC has been cowardly about Palestine and Israel. I've found no takers there for my plans to picket Israeli artists. Some of the Dutch even suggested protesting Arab performers for discriminating against women and preaching violence."

"You are still basically a democrat, Zara," replied Heinz. "Getting people to protest, to act, to vote is something that works only when the situation already has a favorable structure. I can't go into the particulars yet, but if something the countess said is correct, Josh's prospects may include the Levant."

At that moment, as if from another dimension, Herbert appeared with the countess on his arm. One could see that she wore an old-fashioned Olympic tricot swimsuit under her bathrobe. He wore nothing but the glint of moonlight on his skin and what seemed to be a garland on his brow, but it was the shadow of leaves on a tree branch above where he stood. "You look like the marble statue of a Greek god," commented Alex. "Why not?" responded Herby. "It is a timeless fashion."

As none of the tub's occupants made a move to make room for the newcomers, Herby wished them goodnight and so did the countess. Then they were gone as instantaneously as they had arrived. "Zara, that's something you should paint—a classic youth escorting sage dignity," Alex continued. "Do it with a patina that suggests his body could be either flesh or stone and with traces of what she must have looked like when young."

"Sentimental rubbish," responded Zara, "although I must admit she has a good body for her age. Dance training lasts. Come, Alex, it is time to go to bed." Zara clambered out of the tub and wrapped herself in her robe. Alex followed her example good naturedly yet reluctantly. They bid Heinz goodnight. He could now loll in the tub and luxuriate in its space. He relaxed his military rigor and almost drifted into sleep but was kept awake by laughter and chatter from not too nearby but not too far away. Were some of the guests indulging in a hide-and-seek game? As a figure he recognized, Joshua's, approached his tub, the rigor returned to Heinz's torso and limbs.

It was the taut Heinz, the military man at perpetual attention, the Heinz of the master-race mind-set and body tone, who fascinated Joshua. More than having to refute opinions he abhorred, being with this Heinz amounted to constant combat, to strife within. Joshua was fighting himself. He didn't want to find the man sexually magnetic and yet the inklings he had had of another Heinz, the furtive boy, the seminarian who yearned for freedom, were images that for him lacked bite. A Heinz like that was asexual for Joshua. Now, along with the tensions mounting in the man's musculature, besides the firmer set of his jaw and his assertive stare came what for Heinz wasn't mere cant: "This party Herbert has thrown for you suits your decadent side, your Jewness."

"Really? What was it about tonight—the sightseeing, the performance, the many trimmings—that you find particularly Hebraic?"

"That it served as prelude to, as disguise for the frolic going on right now, Herbert's Act 3."

"Granted this whole evening is very Herby, but as far as I can tell, he's not remotely Jewish, rather pagan, no? And, besides, given your games, how can you call Herby's ways decadent? Your preferences may be more one on one, more ritualistic, less a sport, but they can't be any healthier!"

"Ritual is healthier; it purges the emotions and clears the path for finer feelings. Gamesmanship only addicts to more and more insincerity."

Being contradicted excited Heinz. He moved toward Joshua, pulling down the young man's swimming trunks, rapidly removing his own, and then tipping Josh into the water. Heinz steered his own groin against Josh's backside, pushing their upper torsos forward. Joshua hadn't often been penetrated from the rear and didn't enjoy it. He put up enough resistance to further stimulate Heinz, yet let him succeed. After Heinz's climax, he turned Josh sideways, masturbated him, carried him out of the tub, dried him with his own bathrobe, and helped him pull on his trunks.

"Guess we were both being generous tonight," said Josh somewhat out of breath, "because we'll not be together again for a while."

Heinz's retort surprised Joshua. "Why don't we plan to meet in Europe? One of my works is being danced again in Switzerland, and they want me there for rehearsals."

Chapter Fifteen

Mirrors

"Odd that after all these years, the texture hasn't changed, unlike the color," the countess mused as she undid her hair. Her host had escorted her to the door of the bedroom she had been assigned and had bid her goodnight. She had changed into a night gown and seated herself in front of the dressing table mirror, pulled four implements from her overnight bag—a soft brush, a hard brush, a comb of silvery metal, a hand mirror—in preparation for the pre-slumber ritual that had already long ago replaced bedtime prayer in her habits. The countess was proud of her hair's plentitude, particularly its length. She believed that it had never been cut, even when she had been a little girl. Its silvery white sheen now hid no dark shadows—she had been a natural blonde. As she took out the many pins supporting the coiffure that was her daytime crown and as she shook out piled up tresses, her fingers busied themselves separating braids and straightening twists. Then she brushed and again brushed, combed and again combed the profuse strands, interrupting the action ever so often to hold up her small mirror in order to see how her hair looked from the sides and back in the dressing table's large mirror. At her facial features, she hardly glanced. They didn't resemble those of her younger self as much as her hair did, and she had come to accept their matriarchal expressions as endemic. "I must remember to thank Herbert for what he has done. Joshua needed to become aware of his own worth before encountering His Highness."

Once upon a time, the countess, unmarried, had borne a son. She had had to give him up. The boy had been raised by his father, a dashing musician, and by his father's American wife as their joint offspring. It had been the only way to get him out of a Europe on the brink of World War II. Moreover, the wife insisted on being thought of as the boy's blood mother. The countess remained in Middle Europe to nurse her aging, ailing father—a close associate and loyal supporter of the Habsburgs. After her father had died, the countess inherited some of his functions "at court," the unofficial-yet-persistent circle that supported the Habsburg dynasty. "I never felt incomplete not having a husband to care for," she told herself, "but I did need to be a mother. When I met Hertha Heine after the war and she then left Joshua an orphan, my playing mother to him was wonderfully satisfying, even after he was sent away to boarding school in America. The very first letters he ever wrote were to me. It wasn't easy persuading the Habsburgs that I and not a man ought to be his mentor in summer. That he turned out to be gay was a shock. Would it have happened if a man had done the mentoring? I've had to accept Joshua's sexuality as a fact of life, just like the Habsburgs' diminished status. Joshua will never contribute to the family's succession, yet I think he has it in him to have a meaningful life and perhaps rekindle some of the family's glory. If he makes the right impression, if he and His Highness hit it off, I'm convinced he'll be assigned a worthy role."

Chapter Sixteen

Bacchanal

Pulses of summer lightening issue from the horizon, joining the steady moonbeams from overhead to carve shadow shapes such as a romantic painter might conjure out of the vast uniformity of night. Full and closer than at any other time of the year, the moon tonight seems obscenely big and bright. Its nakedness is threatened by a flock of ragged clouds moving in, but this attempt at celestial decency succeeds only intermittently. Throughout the gardens of the hilltop estate, expressions on the faces of Herby's guests are masked by the interplay of darkness and dazzle. Those still partying at this hour must be feeling weary. No telling what they'd been up to earlier in the day. Perhaps some managed a nap prior to boarding the boat. Festivities had started with the early evening cruise through New York's waterways and once past the Statue of Liberty had continued on Staten Island with a drive to the villa. There, attention had to be paid to music and dance. Two repasts had also been on the schedule. Now that bedrooms are being occupied and outdoor bathing is being indulged in, the wine continues to flow. At each pool, sauna, or tub, there are such conveniences as a liquor bar and a cupboard of towels, bathrobes, tissues, and all sorts of sanitary supplies. Herby has begun to make the rounds of the entire property and orders the replenishment of whatever is being used up. At each of the bathing stations, there is a telephone, which he uses to issue instructions. It remains uncertain who receives and carries out his commands to refill ice trays, remove soiled towels and fetch fresh ones, or bring paper and pencil so that names and telephone numbers can be swapped. The guests spot no figures engaged in following orders, but, of course, their attention isn't focused on these practical matters. Only those who have a taste for dallying with the servants are puzzled when they can find none. "They are disguised as guests," concludes one upper-crust, young Brit. Herby himself seems to be turning up everywhere. "He really could tell all," comments Pamela, a young reporter for *The Village Voice* who doesn't feel in the least guilty on this occasion about neglecting her notepad to partake in pleasure.

With some groups dispensing with swimwear, copulations in the water or at its rim aren't infrequent. Herby is careful not to disturb, cautious not to intrude, and tiptoes past. Couples predominate, but there are also threesomes, quartets, and chains—both canny and uncanny. Of course, gender distinctions blur. Watching one configuration is Dr. McCannery. He puffs a fresh cigar and wants to chat with his host. "What an antique scene," he begins. "Certain fashions never go out of date, especially with people believing that they are safer due to improved prevention and hygiene."

"Doesn't there additionally have to be a change of faith? People no longer fear hell's fires as much. Trust in an afterlife and its punishments or rewards is at low ebb. However, as a follower of science's and medicine's prophets, I'm not so certain that all these practices are harmless. With mucous membranes exposed and nerve endings bared, our bodies become ripe for invasion. Right now, we have no bug that can't be dealt with, no disease that can't be prevented. Pubic lice have practically disappeared. There are potent drugs for syphilis and gonorrhea. More tricky are genital ulcers, but they can be guarded against and are still rather rare. Yet nature abhors a vacuum, and who knows whether something new might not evolve or jump its niche to take hold."

"Ah, that's why you are just watching and not indulging."

"No, I'm just slow. Give me time."

"Tonight you may have all the time you want. I'll stall the clocks." Herby replies with a smile as he heads off to the next node and waves the doctor goodnight. The vacant look has come into his eyes but just for an instant.

Chapter Seventeen

Airborne

Joshua loved to travel but hated packing for a trip. He postponed fetching his suitcase and carry-on bag from the storage closet until what for him was the last possible moment—the evening before departing. Deciding what to take, layering the heavier garments into the suitcase, carefully folding them, and lining the folds with tissue paper were tedious processes he carried out with precision. Habitually he would get to bed late that last night at home and yet set the alarm clock for earlier than necessary. By the time he boarded a plane, he'd be overtired. On this trip, he would have had three nights in a row of little sleep before reaching Europe—one due to Herby's party, one due to packing, and one because of sitting awake much of the time on the trans-Atlantic flight from New York. Yet the moment the plane lifted from JFK, the weariness and all travel worries evaporated, leaving his thoughts clear, his feelings fresh, and his senses ready to pounce. At a window seat on the plane's left side (selected in advance so he could see North America's eastern coastline), he was able to look out and watch the beach he had frequented sink away. He noticed too, on his right, the handsome steward who seemed to be giving him the eye from a fold-down seat across the aisle into which he had settled for takeoff. By the time the plane was over Long Island's northern tip and the steward was again patrolling the aisle, they had spoken. Chances, though, were that nothing would come of it. In-flight sex had long been a lure, but commercial planes these days were crowded and cramped. There was barely any opportunity for privacy even after supper was served, darkness dominated outside, the cabin lights were doused, and most passengers were dozing. Turning his thoughts to the imminent future, Joshua considered how he would respond to the family relations who had finally decided to take notice of him. Had the life he was leading in New York been worthwhile enough? That existence gave him freedom without imposing much responsibility. He used the freedom to try to write about art and life, and to maximize his experience of them. The work he had to do because he needed to earn a living wasn't just rote. Translating for the UN exposed him to events, some exceptional, and provided much travel, even some adventure. It was an *Erziehung*, an education, a learning experience many might envy. What, though, was the likelihood that his writing or his existence would matter, would count at all? If he continued that way he would become, at most, just another *Literat* worth a footnote or two in the archives. Did he want to end up a statistic of twentieth-century lifestyles?

On the other hand, if he joined himself to the family, his chances for achieving significance, meaning, worth would be multiplied. It was a singular family, these Habsburgs. They had little real leverage in the contemporary world but gave the impression of much latent power due to what they had once been—*kaiserlich* and *koeniglich* plus canny. As part of that clan, Joshua knew he would have to sacrifice much of his independence. He would have to become circumspect. Appearances would count. Of course, even now flaunting his sexuality at the UN was unacceptable, but no one there bothered being nosy about him. How a minor service official went about scratching his itch wasn't worth an iota of curiosity. A pretender prince's behavior, though, factored. It would be of concern to his family, to the family's fans and stakeholders, to its diverse followers, and to the paparazzi. The countess had cautioned him about the impression he should try to make on the Habsburgs: determined but not totally nonmalleable, temperamentally traditional yet intellectually up to date, and sexually committed to neither matrimony nor the gay life. What they wanted to see would require of Joshua a balancing act. "You are young still," she had reminded him, "still in your early years, so that role shopping ought to come to you naturally. Do it with humor, with ease, and with *Gemuetlichkeit*. Watch yourself as if from the outside and at the same time relax; seem fully engrossed in what you are trying out. Yes, there must be two of you. Both, though, ought to bear the same name— Joshua; Josh must go. To be and not to be, that is the requirement."

Joshua's attention was drawn to a display outside the window. The plane was beginning to turn from its northerly course toward the east. Beyond the left wing, curtains of light became visible in the sky. They were ribbed sheets, pale at first and off white, then differently tinted and shifting like a multilayered theater curtain that gathers into folds in order to entice the eye and seduce the mind into guessing what drama would commence. After he had been watching a while, sleep surreptitiously overcame Joshua, and he awoke just as the flight passed over Norway's coastline and turned south for its destined landing outside Zurich.

He thought of Zurich as a miniature Vienna: Its opera house had been built by the same architects; its older apartment blocks featured similar rows of window frames—each a tiny temple in the classical manner with columns, cornices, pilasters, and pediments—that created the impression of a parade. The Alps were closer to Zurich than to Vienna, and this linguistically German city had almost as many comfortable cafes. It would be a good place to rest and rid himself of jet lag before continuing his journey by rail. He could catch the *Vienna Waltzes*, an express train, to take him east.

Chapter Eighteen

At a Lecture and Later

His Highness was scheduled to visit his ancestral homeland. Austria had been readmitting him since he had renounced a personal and a family claim to the throne. During this stay, he would make his first appearance in public, and the press was paying much attention to the speech he planned to give. It was to be about the idea and the practicality of a united Europe. Joshua wanted to see and hear this bid of his to become a world leader. The young man needed to assess for himself what chances his kinsman, now titled just "Dr.," had for attaining at last something approaching his birthright. Would he be able to embody the concept of being a philosopher king? The initial face-to-face meeting between His Highness and Joshua had been arranged for an hour following the public event.

The location for the lecture couldn't have been more auspicious—it was a venue in Vienna, the Musikverein, named for the Society of the Friends of Music, which had commissioned its construction. The building houses not only the society's offices and meeting rooms but also the city's famed Philharmonic; it is the place in which the orchestra's concerts are held—including the matinee that is broadcast around the globe on New Year's Day. Engineered for superb acoustics and the comfort of the musicians and their audience, the hall of the Musikverein is both harmonious and grand. Joshua dressed as he would for a continental premiere, in a black suit with white shirt; plush blue showed in his tie. It was his first time inside the structure, and he admired its dignified lines, the balconies' declarative angles, the restraint of the gilt plaster, and the glow of the crystal fixtures that hung elongated, like beehives, from overhead. However, the audience that was assembling dismayed him. Although sizeable by Old World standards—all seats would be taken, and there might even be a scarcity of standing room—it seemed an assembly of ancients. Hardly anyone belonged to Joshua's generation or even to several of the preceding ones. The annual rings on brows, under eyes and at the corners of mouths implied a spread from fifty to eighty years. Compared with these people, the ageless caryatids of the wall décor seemed Joshua's contemporaries. There were two types of attendees—ones conservatively well dressed and others in Austrian national garb. At the last moment, a reserved section in front was filled by about twenty older children. Then the houselights dimmed and the stage lit up. A man bustled into view—he seemed wound up in routine—and, stepping up to the microphone, which stood behind baskets of flowers, he began fiddling with its stem and succeeded in lengthening it considerably. He raised the node higher than would have suited him were he to speak. Undoubtedly he was a functionary. Having secured the device and tested it by tapping, he retreated, not having uttered a word. The pause in activity that followed his disappearance served as introduction, as overture, as fanfare for the tall man who stepped out onto the platform and approached the microphone.

What he wore was almost formal afternoon apparel. With composure, he peered at those in the rows in front of him and then seemed to take in the loges and balconies. When he lowered his eyes again, there arose applause. It was substantial. Without having a rhythm or a distinct beat, the sound was measured and considerately slow. The man at the microphone nodded once. Instantly there was silence. That pleased him, and he began to speak. His tone was both authoritative and mellow, and his gestures, although minimal, sufficed to underline major points. Even the least of his motions was clearly dispatched. "This is an emperor, if ever I've seen one!" was the thought that flashed into Joshua's mind.

The topic of uniting Europe also dealt with the thorny issue of winning cooperation from Europe's communist states, including, of course, the Soviet Union. From his proposals for an ideal alliance, the speaker proceeded to raise objections to his own position, but he also allayed such fears. When he ended, he had been thorough yet not excessively long. Nodding once more, he did so smiling this time. Again, as after his entrance, there was applause. It resonated. His Highness had started to turn away and was about to give a goodbye wave when the children in the reserved seats stood and ran up the steps to the platform, bowed or curtsied, and proffered bouquets of flowers, which they wanted to present to him. Turning back to face and thank them, smiling a second time into the spaces of the hall, and with his long arms holding the children's flowers to his chest, he now could go. His walk-off was an affirmation.

Joshua wished that the Countess Zdenka had been present and not back in New York. There was so much he wanted to know about what he had just seen—who had organized the event; more importantly, who had funded it? What did the people in Austrian national costume represent? How sincere and binding was His Highness's renunciation of the throne? It was the countess who had told him that His Highness was still the address for the head of the house among family members and intimates. Was it an ironic or sincere appellation? A box had been filled with men of the collar and one nun. How close was the church to Habsburg ambitions? Joshua wondered how freely he would be able to discuss such things with His Highness himself.

Instructions were that Joshua should call on His Highness an hour after the talk had let out. The older man was staying at the renowned Imperial, a hotel in walking distance of the Musikverein, and there wasn't really enough time for Joshua to repair to his own modest hotel in the Second District, so he strolled along the Ring boulevard, looking at shop windows, peering into cafes and restaurants, watching the streetcars swing past, and observing humanity. The Viennese habitually spent much of their leisure time out and about. Seldom did they entertain anyone but close family at home. One would be invited to one's host's regular coffeehouse and could sit there chatting for hours while consuming very little drink or food. It was a custom that had survived countless wars and domestic crises, and Joshua noticed that even the most rebellious of the young generation kept up the practice.

When Joshua presented himself at the Imperial, the reception-ist phoned His Highness's suite and then informed Joshua that he was invited to go upstairs. Exiting from the elevator at the designated floor, he turned a corner into a long, well-lit, softly carpeted hallway and was head-ing toward a number that likely was at the corridor's far end when a door there opened and several persons emerged and walked toward him. It was a diverse group, men and women, young and old, yet all well dressed and seeming somehow related. As Joshua passed them, they did not take particular note of him. "My presence here hasn't been announced to the family," he thought to himself, "and it won't be unless I pass scrutiny." He knocked at the door he had been sent to; it was the one from which the group had exited, and after a moment, it was opened by a woman who enjoined him to enter. Her manner, Joshua thought, was as casually commanding as that of any guardian for the UN's great heads of state. She was perhaps a decade older than Joshua, and was dressed almost like the women he had passed in the hallway yet a little more officially. If she hadn't worn her tailored summer suit like a uniform, one might have counted her as quite comely. She introduced herself as His Highness's secretary, Andrea Amundsen-Lemortzin, inquiring when he had arrived in Vienna and where he was staying. The latter information she noted down. She was about to ask him to take a seat in the room, which appeared to be outer office and reception space in one, when an inner door opened. His Highness stood there, and Joshua again was impressed by how tall and upright he appeared to be. His stature hadn't been a theatrical illu-sion. For a minute that seemed to last longer than clocks tick the time, the two relatives looked at each other. The senior one's stare was military at first—with such eyes and brows a commanding general might appraise a new force appearing on the battlefield and try to ascertain whether it was friend or foe. The junior one met that gaze without a qualm and suc-ceeded in transforming his opposite's severity into a sort of welcome. "So, you are our nephew, my long dead brother's son grown up. I once saw you, briefly, when you were still a tot." His Highness spoke in lightly accented American English, having spent some of the World War II years among citizens of the United States.

"Yes, I've grown up, my mother's son as well as my father's, I suspect, but the result too of my teachers and circumstance," Joshua replied, not without humor in his slightly old-fashioned, somewhat childlike Viennese German. "It won't do really to accuse any of them. In the end, I have only myself to blame for what I've become."

"You are still becoming, it seems to me, and it is much too soon to mention blame or praise. I wish I had as many years ahead as you will have. I didn't know your mother, but my brother, who was young and brave, loved her. I only heard about your teachers and a few other factors in your life from our friend, the Countess Zdenka. I would like to get to know you a little. I hope you have the time now to start things off. Perhaps you'll also want to get to know me somewhat. Shall we talk?"

They had been standing, and Frl. Andrea asked whether they wanted to go into the next room, which served as His Highness's inner office, and should she bring them something to drink or eat. Did they want *Jause*?

"No, no. Not here. I've not been out all day and need to walk. Do you mind, Joshua? We'll stroll a bit and then could sit down at a café. Here we'll just be interrupted." In fact, the telephone on Frl. Andrea's desk had been ringing constantly, and she had switched it to automatic answering.

It was a pleasant evening for walking, the streets still daylit and the air temperate. His Highness's long legs and determination made him a fast companion. Joshua had to keep up the rapid pace that, once set, was barely altered, and he realized it was expected that he would also keep up his end of what might turn out to be an exacting conversation. He was being tested—not only about his life but also about his awareness and responses to the chance sights, sounds, and smells they were encountering on their outing. From the Imperial, they crossed the Ring and headed into the narrow streets of the inner city. Historic houses squeezed shoulders with current constructions and with hybrids of past and present. "That compromise, how does it strike you?" Joshua was asked about a modernized storefront that served as base for several stories of an eighteenth-century façade. He replied with considered taste. Measures from an aria by Mozart issued onto the sidewalk as they passed a café, and there followed the query whether Joshua had acquired the Viennese habit for opera. His response alluded to his love of ballet. From an open window in which a lace curtain waved came the tangy aroma of bakery. His Highness, glancing sideways at Joshua, commented that he seemed to have the sensitive Habsburg nose, and it appeared to be unspoiled by smoking. These interjections were made while the main topic of their exchange was the Countess Zdenka. "She is fiercely self sufficient in the face of growing old. And beginning to need a little looking after."

"I'm trying to do that without it showing. She is the closest thing I've known to having a mother."

Joshua was passing His Highness's probes of his alertness and loyalty. How much history did he know, particularly family history? As they passed a newly plastered, painted, and trimmed edifice boasting big, freshly varnished wooden doors that stood open on a balconied inner courtyard, His Highness commented on how well the pots of orange flowers on the balconies went with the color of the building's plaster—a golden mustard, in fact the Maria Theresia yellow. Joshua asked whether this *palais* wasn't or hadn't been in possession of the Liechtensteins, a noble family intermarried with the Habsburgs.

"Alliances exist. Habsburgs are joined to the Lorraines, the Luxembourgs, Liechtensteins, and a legion of other elevated families. Sometimes these links help, and sometimes they hinder. At least the Liechtensteins have regained a little of their wealth, influence, and sense of duty."

"And how do you see that, the sense of duty?"

"A good question, as they say on radio talk programs. At minimum, it is to set an example by one's self and with one's family, an example of service to humanity. I don't mean one has to discover, invent, or create. Those are fine gifts if you have them, but few do. Yet to live a civilized life, to lead a little where there are uncertainties, moral vacuums, or even where there is stifling anomie, that is something most people could do but don't. There seem to be fewer and fewer who find the time to spare from the immediate, practical matters of earning a living. Civilization, especially since the last world war, seems to be debasing the human character. A few families, though, still cultivate humane values. The Habsburgs have lost their lands, their legions, their crowns, and their throne. Yet there is still among us a sense of family, of duty. People recognize us for it. Much of my time is spent answering requests. It strains our funds, but I don't like to say no. Actually, it is easier to deny giving help when one's resources are unlimited. As a poor man, I have a hard time denying appeals since saying yes will not cost me money anyway, only effort and time."

They had passed the Cabaret Ronacher and were on Weihburggasse approaching the Franciscan church when His Highness stopped a moment to suggest that they avoid the busy Kaertnerstrasse and instead should cut in back of St. Stephen's to the arcades that parallel another major artery, Rotenturmstrasse. First, though, he wanted to step into the *Franciskanerkirche* for a glimpse of its old baroque organ. Luck was with them, for the organist was practicing a fugue. His Highness had crossed himself after entering; Joshua had not and was asked about his faith. "I am an atheist, the old-fashioned sort," he replied.

"Please explain what you mean by that. There have been rabid atheists throughout history, as militant as any Inquisition Jesuit."

"I'm the mild sort, with tolerance for what people imagine whether it be Jupiter or Jesus. Jocasta has the reality of potent fiction in people's minds. She survives as a concept from culture to culture for countless generations and will win no matter how much censorship a Mme. Mao may connive. To deny people their god or gods is as futile as forbidding art."

"I, unlike you, young man, believe in the God of the Catholic Church because I believe in my family. That does not mean that I approve of all the church does. I've known priests who try to be too holy and those convinced they must be sinners in order to experience forgiveness. As a simple man, I try to avoid both those sorts. Your atheism doesn't seem to me extreme, and I'm glad you mentioned it only upon my asking. The priests you may meet at my dinner table aren't likely to be swirling red capes in front of your eyes." The implication that he might be admitted to the inner circle did not go unnoticed by Joshua.

Having emerged from the shopping arcades, they were approaching the Danube Canal, again avoiding the major artery named for a Red Tower razed long ago, but along narrow little streets that veined their way through the inner city's northeast. Crossing the canal on its Swedish Bridge, they cut to their right and before entering Prater Street, stopping to admire the elaborate window rows of a nineteenth-century building at the sharp corner of Great Moor Lane. A little further on, they paused to look at the playwright Nestroy's likeness and considered whether they should take a table at the café behind the statue. His Highness decided no, that instead they would proceed to the Prater ("… that's a park there …" as the song in English goes) and sit under some of its chestnut trees that would still be in full leaf though long past their colorful flowering (celebrated in a local hit tune).

Quite a bit of striding would remain before they reached the park. By the time they crossed the *etoile* with Admiral Tegetthoff's column, hub of several radial avenues and trolley lines, had passed under the viaduct of the Rail North Station, and emerged in the park, Joshua had been questioned about his knowledge of Austrian military history, geography, and law. He was deficient in the first, but thanks to his UN assignments and his own curiosity, it was with flying colors that he passed His Highness's tests about Imperial land claims and the liberality of Franz Josefian legal reforms. Once in the Prater, His Highness decided they would avoid the louder pleasure park with its rides, booths, and beer gardens, which were beginning to be lit up for the nighttime hours. Instead, they headed into the more sylvan section and chose to seat themselves at an outdoor table of a quietly comfortable establishment. A light supper seemed right. After ordering, the topic of conversation, of examination, was turned to ballet, which Joshua had earlier said he loved.

"What do you know about Clementine Kraus?" asked His Highness.

"She was a leading mime during the Hassreiter era at the ballet here."

"Correct, but that reply doesn't begin to tell all. Freulein Kraus was a beautiful woman of a distinct type. In the eyes of the public, she represented the Viennese girl of that time—lots of charm yet proud, smart, and beginning to be independent. She knew how to infuse those qualities into her roles, whether she was cast as a goddess or villainess. Moreover, she was related to the Vetseras and through them had entrée to court society. Clementine Kraus became a favorite of the emperor's, and he made her his eyes and ears within his ballet company. Its style and Hassreiter's creations were things he sanctioned. He could be budged on points of foreign policy but never on what ought to be the ballet's look and manner. "Joshua was able to talk about the pre-World War 1 productions he knew of, works with simple or sumptuous titles such as *At the Hair Salon*, *Roundabout Vienna*, *Sun and Earth*, *Vienna Waltzes*, and the single actual survivor, *The Fairy Doll*. When their food arrived, His Highness continued with "Franz Josef was very exacting. Everything labeled Imperial Royal received his attention. He knew the privileges and obligations that came with each of his many inherited titles and kept a list of the measures he had taken in their regard. Everyone, of course, knows that as emperor, king, or in some other princely capacity, he ruled Austrian, Hungarian, Bohemian land and, too, Balkan and Polish soil. Yet there were odd legacies also, such as King of Lodomeria and King of Jerusalem."

Joshua wondered what and where in the world Lodomeria was and learned that likely it was Russian territory abutting Polish Galicia. The Jerusalem claim derived from the Crusades. Could it have been bestowed on Richard the Lionhearted, who on his way home to Britain had relinquished it to his temporary Austrian host and captor? "That title has become actual again," concluded His Highness, "but it is getting too late to relate the circumstances now. Perhaps I'll tell the story at the dinner party I'm inviting you to the day after tomorrow. I trust you can attend. Freulein Andrea will let you know where and when." His Highness settled their bill, had the waiter signal a taxi, and asked Joshua whether he might drop him at his hotel. Declining with thanks, Joshua bid His Highness goodnight and was about to reach out his hand when the tall man's hand came down on his left shoulder. "I am happy to have met you, nephew, and look forward to next time." When the hand lifted from Joshua's shoulder, it felt—and he could also see the action as if observing it from outside himself—like a sword in a knighting ceremony being raised.

Chapter Nineteen

Little Tables, Lots of Kin

It was more than a dinner party that His Highness had arranged. Weather permitting, wine and *Broetchen* would be served on the steep and shaded lawn of Princess Marianne's villa in suburban Doebling. The meal would then take place indoors. Joshua was aware of all His Highness hadn't asked him on their walk. The young man's profession and career prospects, the status of his citizenship and ties to America, and of course his personal liaisons were aspects that had to factor in the family's assessment of him. Undoubtedly, His Highness already possessed certain information from the Countess Zdenka, perhaps also from other sources. He would want, however, to know to what it amounted, and for that Joshua's own choice of words and selection of tone were crucial. Still, was it likely that these topics would be broached at a gathering, even a family one? No, Joshua was sure that the purpose of this party was to test his social fitness and see how the family took to him.

Princess Marianne, co-hostess of the occasion, had already taken a dislike to Joshua. It wasn't an instant one but a constitutional rejection. Frl. Andrea had predicted that would be the case because he was single, eligible, rather American, above all he was a relative not obliged to the family in any way. This sort of individual went against the Princess's grain. To her, acknowledged kinship with such a person spelled trouble.

Joshua had studied Frl. Andrea's guest list. It had been annotated for him very carefully, and as His Highness took him around on the lawn to meet all the men, imparting additional information on occasion—that this uncle was still in mourning for his wife, that that cousin would soon announce his betrothal, that Cousin Martha's spouse was the family's art authority—the ostensible responses to meeting him were mixtures of reserved courtesy and polite curiosity. It seemed clear from His Highness's affable manner that he was kindly disposed to Joshua, and no one other than Princess Marianne was being querulous. She ought to have but didn't introduce him to the women. They took pity on him and came up in twos or threes to introduce themselves. More among them than Joshua anticipated were prominent professionals. Cousin Christina, a young astronomer, he found particularly simpatica.

Small tables, twelve of them, had been placed in the villa's many windowed, ground-floor rooms. Each table was set for six, yet with only four place cards. Genders had segregated spontaneously on the lawn, but the indoor seating was mixed although not necessarily by household. The reason for the pair of empty places at each table was so that His Highness and Joshua could table hop. How accustomed His Highness was to this arrangement became apparent. He was a master at ending conversations by tucking in any loose corners, raising his wine glass or water tumbler with a no-drop-spilled flourish as he rose from his chair, turning to the next table, and there adroitly inserting himself and Joshua into whatever the topic of conversation had been. Then he would conjure a bridge to something he wanted to talk about. At first, table switching hit Joshua like a jolt, but he adjusted.

Questions about Joshua's life did arise—not directly, but under the guise of what was New York like now, had it truly become the nexus for lifestyles, the world's culture capital and trial court for testing ideas. Quite a few family members had visited New York, and there were those who had to go there repeatedly on business. Joshua covered his intimacy with the high life and low life as part and parcel of his translator's job and of his moonlighting as an arts writer.

A latecomer to the dinner was a nun, the one who had sat in the box with the male clerics at the Musikverein. She was not old, but Joshua couldn't guess how young she might be, and he didn't recall seeing her name on the guest list. His Highness addressed her simply as Gertrude.

The three others at this table were siblings, two brothers and their sister. His Highness joked, after he and Joshua had seated themselves for the dessert course, that it was sweet to be among single people in their prime. Gertrude reminded him that she considered herself wed, a bride of Christ. Outspoken, not at all shy, she was in fact a psychiatrist, engaged in studying the ramifications of religious celibacy. "I understand that our American priesthood has a rather loose definition of sex. They consider it something done with women that they have vowed to avoid, but that it is an entirely different story when it comes to indulging in it with each other and with boys," she said provocatively while scooping up whipped cream with her fork. Clearly uncomfortable with the topic, the other woman at the table had begun to frown. Gertrude was looking at Joshua quizzically, but before he had even decided how to respond, His Highness intervened.

"Celibacy, like the other religious vows, is voluntary. It has always been so in theory, but today it is so in practice too. A young person who finds himself or herself unsuited to one or all of the three principal vows can always return to the profane life."

Gertrude's "Really?" was sharp.

The elder of the brothers, as if emerging from a daydream, asked Joshua about the churchgoing habits of American Catholics, the younger one wanted to know about Catholic-Protestant ecumenical relations in America, and by then their sister had recovered enough to comment on how peculiar she had found it in America that the church towers weren't taller—in fact they were often shorter—than secular buildings. Celibacy and sex were not mentioned again. Joshua concluded this, the last sitting, with a yarn about his seeking out gospel choirs in New York's Harlem. When everyone was standing and coffee had been served, His Highness asked Joshua to repeat the story because "you describe the voices so well. You ought to move to Vienna and be a music critic." It was clear to all assembled that the long lost American's chances of being fully adopted into the family were fairly good.

Joshua's tests, though, weren't over. The dinner party led to a flurry of other smaller invitations. Cousin Martha's husband gave him a tour of

Vienna's private art galleries, which were just beginning to reopen for their autumn shows. Cousin Christina drove him to the observatory at which she was a staff appointee and explained how astronomers were proposing to find planets around other suns once new and better-situated telescopes were in operation. The three single siblings suggested a night out at the theater, perhaps for one of Grillparzer's plays, which they doubted he had ever sat through in New York. Also a number of his older relations invited him to *Jause* at home or at their favorite café or *Konditorei*. To Joshua's surprise, it was the Princess Marianne, crossing paths with him at His Highness's suite in the Imperial, who brought an invitation from Gertrude to a lecture she was giving. Joshua thanked the princess for being messenger and remarked, pointedly, on how graciously she had extended herself to host the dinner party that had introduced him to the family. His Highness smiled broadly, pleased that Joshua was keeping score and letting the princess know. However, he asked Joshua to not attend the lecture. This angered the princess and led to an exchange of words—brief but clear as swordplay. It was the first time Joshua had witnessed discord between two Habsburgs.

The grades given Joshua's deportment on the several family occasions were more than passing. His Highness joked about the young man's excellent report card. Two critical "exams," however, remained—a meeting with His Highness's best friends and one with His Highness's church advisors. Neither session had yet been scheduled. As ever, though, time was a tension not readily relaxed: Joshua's vacation leave was due to expire, so he informed His Highness.

"Apply for an extension and give urgent family concerns as the reason," His Highness suggested. "I have enough influence still that your request will be granted." It was, and without the usual bureaucratic delay. What may have motivated Joshua's UN bosses was that no decision had been made as to where his translator skills would be required in the foreseeable future. Placing a translator wasn't just a minor administrative matter. In dicey situations, it had happened that the UN translator turned out to be more than a technician, serving also as diplomat and peacemaker when not a single delegate present stepped forward to take on the leadership role. In any case, it was with that in mind that Josef Levitan, chief UN translator and also an eminent dance critic, trained and placed his staff. Joshua was one of Levitan's star pupils. The longer leave, it turned out, would serve not just the UN and His Highness. It would also allow Joshua to take the trip to Salonika he had been contemplating so that he might see his birthplace with adult eyes. First, though, he decided to enjoy himself a little, to have a real vacation and indulge in Vienna's versions of fleshpots.

Chapter Twenty

At the Baths

The year 1969 had been symbolic for sensuality. Dionysus's worshipers and their fervid friends continued to celebrate throughout the decade that followed. Dominant in these revels was the gay faction. Heterosexuals or bisexuals were followers in such matters, not leaders. Still, Vienna's sensuality had a comfortably orderly aura; it was *artig und gemuetlich*. For pickups, the principal spots were cafes or bars. As long as the good weather lasted—this was a sunny September—outdoor locations thrived: parts of the Prater and certain other parks, bathing beaches such as the Gaensehaeufel (Gooseheap) along the Old Danube, some clearings in the nearby Vienna Woods. All these places, though, were public, and the Countess Zdenka had urged Joshua to be discreet, so he decided on an indoor baths where there was no chance of being seen by uninvolved observers. Several "men's baths" were listed in the telephone directory, the majority sporting Graeco-Roman names—from Apollo to Zeus. He chose the Hermesbad. Its founding dated back, according to its phone book ad, to before World War I—1908 to be precise, the 60th year of Franz Josef's reign and also the year of the great modernist art show in his honor that he tolerated.

Venerable though it was, the Hermesbad had just been plushly restored. It was situated near the snack market, the Naschmarkt—Vienna's outdoor collection of stalls and booths for the finest farm produce and prepared foods. Joshua found the address to be that of an apartment house, a rather anonymous one on the outside, but on the inside, the baths occupied half the cellar, an eighth of the ground floor and, skipping several stories, a quarter of the building's top floor. There was also a roof garden for sunbathing.

A two-winged entrance door from the building's parterre passageway bore just a small enamel sign with the establishment's name. Joshua pressed the bell button next to the sign, heard a click, and pushed open the right half of the door. He found himself in a wood paneled vestibule, facing a cashier's window. No one was behind the window, though, so he waited. Calling out a hello after a while, he heard his query answered by a mezzo male voice remarking on his hurry. "It will be just as nice, perhaps nicer, if you give it time." There appeared an unnaturally blond fellow, about Joshua's age, very muscled in his tight T-shirt and carrying a stack of clean towels, which he deposited at one end of the cashier's counter. Turning to Joshua, he said, "Good afternoon," and asked, "How can I help you?

"I would like to have a sauna."

"Only a sauna? How about a massage too?"

"Perhaps, but let me decide about that later."

"Likely you'll make out with a volunteer, but in case not you can make your own arrangements then with one of our staff masseurs." There was little of the pretense now that had persisted in gay establishments long after World War II about this being just a spot for Vienna's sportsmen. "By the way, do you want a room, a cubicle, or a cabinet?"

Joshua decided to splurge and asked for a room. It was pricey. He paid his bill, again heard a click, and noticed a second door at the far end of the vestibule swing open. Through it, he stepped into a large, luxurious lounge. Daylight filtered in at the far end through partly opaque panes of whorled glass. Most of the illumination, though, came from a scattering of lamps—some on low tables next to sofas and ottomans, others suspended from the ceiling—creating islands of brightness in a lagoon of shadows. The parquet floor was partly covered by small Persian rugs. Paintings, many of them, hung on the two walls perpendicular to the one with windows. The pictures' heavy gilt frames glowed like dying embers in this light. Joshua wondered whether the collection might stem from painters involved in the 1908 show, but it was too dim to see much detail. One canvas he could make out depicted a Homeric landscape, and another was, possibly, an urban perspective a la Sappho, but these two specimens certainly weren't modernist but rather Biedermeier. Joshua, though, wasn't about to strain his eyes on the rest of the collection or ask whether the lighting could be turned up. Well lit and parallel to the wall opposite the windows, a bar had been installed. It was stocked with bottles, drinking glasses and with a handsome bartender who stood behind the counter. He kept wielding a moist cloth to clean, unnecessarily, the marble countertop while chatting with his only customer, a middle-aged man wrapped in a big towel and perched on one of the high stools in front of the bar. They spoke in hushed tones. Apart from the voices of these two, only the barely audible sound of music, waltz music, issuing from a hidden radio enhanced the impression of a great silence. There were several others in the lounge, but they were resting, each by himself, on the comfortable furniture for that purpose. It was early afternoon outside, and yet here it seemed past bedtime. The recumbent young bodies and relaxed features of these patrons appeared drained of desire. Two of them looked up appraisingly as Joshua entered, but among the remainder there reigned utter passivity, or at most there was the tucking-in of a towel that had become unwrapped. A jaded, enervated, harem ambience pervaded the space.

Josh had paused in the lounge to orient himself and examine the room key he had been given. It didn't take him long to spot a sign indicating that private rooms were on the top floor. To reach them, one had to ascend several stories, and for that the Hermesbad had a curious antique—a contraption dubbed a *pater noster* by Catholic Vienna. It was an early alternative to the single cabin, manually operated elevator and consisted of boxes narrow as coffins but open, lacking a lid. These boxes stood one atop the other, toe to head, and moved continuously through two shafts, up one and down the other. To be transported to another floor, one had to jump in and out quickly because the coffins never paused. That frightened people, so they said their *pater noster* prayer as they jumped.

Joshua, getting in on the ground floor, giggled but wondered whether he'd be turned upside down if he failed to jump out at the next opening, the top floor, and decide to give it a try. No, after passing that level, his coffin ascended to what must have been the attic where there was no opening, moved sideways smoothly without upending, and descended the twin shaft. He jumped out as he passed the top floor a second time.

Small though the private rooms were, the bed was big and filled almost the entirety of the space. Joshua's room had, to his surprise, a window that, when he opened the curtains, gave him a view over rooftops and let in light to show clean linens on his bed, unblemished paint (the Maria Theresia yellow) on the walls and even a solitary work of art (a small cubist still life) opposite the door that opened out. He undressed, placing his belongings in a narrow, lockable cupboard that stood in one corner, put on the white bathrobe of toweling that had been supplied and went out to explore. Most of the rooms seemed locked, unoccupied as yet. A circular metal stair led to the open roof, which had sunbathing benches, flower boxes and gave wide vistas on the city and on distant hilltops. When he returned to the hallways of the top floor after having lingered on the roof to soak up the late summer sun, a few room doors stood open, but Joshua didn't feel like investigating these invitations. He descended by *pater noster* past the ground floor opening to the cellar level where there was a large exercise studio, a sauna, a dry hot room, showers, and toilets. Everything seemed pristine. For a while he used an exercycle and was engaged in small talk by a chap with a Slavic accent who was doing stretches and bends on a gym mat nearby. He seemed barely out of his late teens, and Joshua surmised that he was a refugee from Communist terrain trying to make a living as a Vienna call boy. "The management here admits only those of us they've found to be reliable," he boasted. Joshua did not bid on the lad's offer but gave him a friendly goodbye and went to the main floor lounge to rest.

It must have gotten to be after 3 p.m. Joshua didn't have his watch with him, and the only clock he had seen was out in the entrance vestibule, but more customers had arrived. It was an attractive clientele. He went back into the cellar to try the sauna, hanging his robe on a hook outside the heavy door and entering nude. Steam swirled inside, and there was but little light. Of course that made it difficult to ascertain anything with just one's eyes, but as Joshua carefully made his way into the interior, it was obvious that others were using their hands in order to see who might be passing by. Wooden platforms rose stepwise from a tiled floor toward the sauna's ceiling. Human shapes, sitting upright or lounging, dotted the platforms. Joshua found a spot not near anyone else and occupied it. As his vision adjusted to the dense, dim atmosphere, he noticed the source of the steam, a metallic oven that stood against one wall halfway back into the sauna. On its surface, there were elaborate arrays of holes and vents from which jets and geysers of vapor escaped into the sauna room. He also became aware of the platform farthest from the entrance door. On it, there was an aggregate, a tangle of bodies that looked like the Laocoon statue multiplied, moistened, and moving with a rhythmic pulse. Audible in the sauna were the sounds of steam hissing, water dripping from the ceiling onto the tile floor, and people exhaling. Once in a while, there issued from the massed bodies someone's ecstatic moan, and then there followed the echo of affirmation from a chorus—"Ja, ja, ja!"

On his platform, Joshua kept himself occupied by peering at the tangle, picking out enticing body parts, and imagining how it would be to embrace that trim torso, clasp that muscled arm, or pump that penis. When someone was about to reach climax, Joshua's eyes became glued to his face, to its features, to its every change of expression. Was there any better way to know, to understand, to sense another individual, and to do it without merging, without losing oneself, without experiencing a little death than by witnessing the other's orgasm? Perhaps for Joshua, there was a different, an equal, an alternate way—instances when he had focused on a dancer negotiating substantial choreography. The scrutiny in such circumstances disclosed as much feeling, challenge, choice, thought, and determination, and revealed the point at which generosity and privacy pivoted, confessed it as precisely as did an individual's behavior during sex. He pondered these situations and also wondered why he wanted the experience, wanted it over and over again. What Joshua hadn't, though, at least did not have then and there, was the urge to actually join in, to immerse himself in that upholstered mass of sensing skin, so he remained seated, some distance off, chin resting on his drawn up knees and arms wrapped around his shins.

Not only were steam and heat making Joshua sweat profusely, but he was also becoming drowsy. To doze off in the sauna wasn't a good idea, so he got up and went to a spot near the door where a cold water hose could be turned on and off. He hosed himself down, returned to where he had been sitting and resumed observing the tangle. Like an amoeba, it bulged sometimes in one direction and then in another, but maintained its integrity remarkably considering that individuals kept joining it or departing. How long was its lifespan—hours, or, since the Hermesbad was never shut, could it endure for days? Might it be that this living statue was eternal? Drowsiness was again overcoming Joshua, and he nodded off briefly. Someone sitting down on his platform at very close quarters roused him. Not a bad specimen, it turned out. Joshua was being stared at intensely, and then he was being touched. A hand had reached out. Joshua leaned over toward this inquisitive neighbor and placed his own hand on the young man's shoulder, smiled, and shook his head "no." He had come here for dalliance, either mass action or one-on-one, but not right now. The young man moved on to someone on another platform, and Joshua again began watching the tangle. In it, two adjacent profiles caught his attention. Despite the curtains of vapor and the low lighting, Joshua thought he recognized Herbert and Heinz. Someone with dark hair was suckling Herbie's right nipple while Herbie's left arm was thrown around the neck of Heinz, who was massaging the groin of the body to his left—an individual as blond as he but seemingly more supple. The suckler and the supple one were soon replaced, yet the presumed Herbie and Heinz remained together in the stirrings of the fleshpot.

What were they up to, these two, coming to Vienna? Having had sex separately with both, he oughtn't to be jealous of their having gotten together for a communal indulgence. Why, though, hadn't they let him know of their presence in town? To accost them while they were part of the tangle was out of the question, so Joshua decided to wait in the shower area outside the sauna. He washed, put on his robe, sat on a bench, and then sat waiting. They didn't come out. Going back in, he found the tangle had indeed persisted, but neither Herbert nor Heinz belonged to it any longer. He searched the rest of the sauna to no avail. Had they exited while he was showering? Possible but unlikely, and wouldn't they too have wanted to wash off? Joshua explored the entire Hermesbad from basement to roof garden. There was no sign of them. Of course, there were private rooms with locked doors he couldn't enter. He described Herbie and Heinz to the attendant in the vestibule as best he could, and was told that several people looking like either one or the other had checked in or out separately, but there had been no such pair together.

Joshua went to his room, dressed, checked out, and returned to his hotel, walking all the way from the Naschmarkt to the Praterstern. The air felt ever so fresh on the steam purged skin of his face and hands. Had he imagined Herbert and Heinz? Was he beginning to miss his New York life and friends? As for the pleasure he hadn't had that afternoon, he told himself that there would be time enough for it in the future.

Chapter Twenty One

At the Abbey

Upriver from Vienna, the Danube bends baroquely between high hills and low mountains. Vineyards slope down the hillsides to the water's edge, and castles fallen into ruin straddle the sheer crests. At a crossing in this region known as the Wachau Valley, an Augustinian abbey, Stift Duernstein, was built once upon a time. Now the abbey was just the church of a pastoral precinct, but it and its attendant buildings were well maintained and served as a center for conferences, religious, and otherwise. This was the place that had been picked for His Highness to present Joshua to select members of the Catholic Church hierarchy.

It was a seductive September morning when His Highness and Joshua set out for the meeting in a sports car Frl. Andrea had arranged for them. Joshua was doing the driving, and they decided to keep the top down. Even with the wind in their ears, His Highness felt obliged for Joshua's sake to ruminate further about his and the family's relations to the church. "There is nothing official now, but habit and traditions can be more powerful than legal proclamations or signed and sealed declarations," he began to explain and then stopped. After a pause, he started again, "It was custom for the House of Habsburgs to obtain church approval for what it undertook on its own initiative. Even privileges won outright through warfare or diplomacy used to be submitted for church approval because that would then prompt popular assent. Other activities, though, came to the family as duties, obligations, assignments. For instance, the title of Holy Roman Emperor. It was a papal invention, bestowed on one of our ancestors and passed down ever since. It helped immensely to have a faith above nationhood as moral authority when we united Germanics, Magyars, Slavs, Latins, and others into one empire. It was even an advantage in dealing with other faiths—the Orthodox churches, Jews, Muslims. Perhaps not with Protestants."

"How current, though, is any of that?" Joshua asked. "And didn't the Catholic Church's involvement in worldly affairs ignite the Reformation and ultimately limit its hegemony?"

"Some of the Church's meddling was brilliant and beneficial. Other deeds were devious and divisive. Which of the thousand years of Vatican-Habsburg history do you, my dear young atheist, wish to discuss? That the church did not meddle, did not take measures to stop castration practices, the slave trade, or Nazi concentration camps has been criticized as much as has its involvement in the world. You are wrong, however, to think that it has all turned to cobwebs and dust, that now it is nothing more than old history, just politics of the past. I am faced with a present problem, a current concern that crosses religious, national, and cultural gaps. I didn't seek it out. It landed in my lap, thanks to my church given title, King of Jerusalem."

"You mentioned that once before but postponed telling me the particulars," Joshua said. "I know you are heir to many crowns, but how in the world could such a title still be current?"

"It has taken rabbinical thinking to revive it. You work for the UN, so you must be aware that Jerusalem is a disputed place. Is it to be the capital of Israel or of a Palestinian state, of both or of neither? That quandary, as insoluble and all consuming as it may prove to be, is not the only one involving the sacred city. Have you ever visited there? No! Jerusalem is fascinating. It is a magnet for all sorts of faiths—the major forms of Judaism, Christianity, and the Muslim religion as well as their variants. One group of Jews, a minority but not negligible, consists of those who take the Bible's and the Talmud's texts literally. These fundamentalists, these ultra-Orthodox Jews believe that there can be a Jewish state only when the Messiah comes. According to all Jews, the Messiah has not yet come, and so the ultra-Orthodox among them refuse to recognize Israel, its laws and regulations, and its jurisdiction over their Jerusalem neighborhoods. Muslims, of course, are delighted by that stance. Christians are confused by the situation, even Christians who are staunchly fundamentalist. Israel ignores the insults and complaints hurled against it by the ultra-Orthodox Jews but takes no measures against them, in fact protects them. The ultra-Orthodox don't want that; they reject being nannied by those they see as being irreligious co-religionists, yet they have come to acknowledge their need for a temporal ruler. He would also be a temporary one, until the Messiah appears, and he must not be a Jew because then he might be construed as a false messiah, become accursed and bring the wrath of God on those he rules. It has come to pass, as the sacred scribes might say, that the ultra-Orthodox rabbinate petitioned the UN to send them the proper person for this task—the individual who is heir to the historic title King of Jerusalem, and that is me."

The thought that history is prone to repeat its pranks occurred to Joshua. The absurdity of a crusade had linked the Habsburgs and Jerusalem once upon a time and now the absurdities of ultra-Orthodoxy, nationalism, conversion, misalliance were linking them again. He shot a glance at His Highness. As usual, his uncle's features seemed calmly in command, with a slight crease in the right corner of his mouth, a smile that may have been elicited by the situation he had been explaining or by the lovely landscape through which they were driving.

The rest of the way, which wasn't long, passed in relative silence, although on occasion His Highness pointed out a historic site or a noteworthy winery. When they saw the blue and white tower of the Duernstein church, it looked from Rossatz, on the Danube's opposite bank, like a ladder between river and sky. They crossed the Danube by ferry.

In the building nestling to the left of the church's tower, a room had been reserved for the meeting. They were ushered into the house, up a staircase, and into the room by a motherly woman wearing an apron—a lay person, apparently the matron of the concierge's family. She departed, closing the door. They were alone in a large space into which sunlight streamed through one of the windows. The ceiling above them was high, and in the center of the floor stood a long oval table with chairs, straight-backed ones. Book cases lined the walls except at the entrance door and where there were windows—there were many windows on two opposite sides of the room. One set looked into a courtyard, and the other overlooked the Danube. Over the table hung a metal chandelier, and between the table and the walls, there was ample pacing space. The flooring was wood, broad planks, without any covering of mats or rugs. His Highness and Joshua were about to either pace or examine books on the shelves when, precisely as the church tower sounded the third stroke of ten o'clock, the door to the room opened, admitting a small assembly of men. Joshua counted twelve. They were clerically dressed but not all identically, some having dark suits with the stiff white collar of separation whereas others wore cassocks of which a couple differed in color from black. Two elderly figures were foremost. The majority, Joshua thought, were between forty and sixty. The last to enter was the youngest, perhaps Joshua's age. It was he who closed the door.

His Highness approached the pair of elders, shook hands with them but addressed everyone. "Thank you, gentlemen, for disrupting your schedules and taking the time to meet with us. What we are here to discuss is a request, an appeal from another faith, one that may have consequences for our church whether it is granted or not. First, though, please let us sit down so that we can make introductions in an orderly and more comfortable manner." For himself, he chose a chair near the middle of the table with the windows facing the Danube behind him. To Joshua, he indicated the opposite spot "because, gentlemen, he and I will speak and you will question." Everyone, even the elders, quickly found a place, yet the introductions took time. Again, His Highness was first. "Not that any of you are in doubt, but I am Otto Habsburg, Dr. Habsburg, formerly von Habsburg, and still head of the family that once ruled Austria-Hungary and the Holy Roman Empire. As far as Austria-Hungary is concerned, I have relinquished all imperial and royal claims. Some claims, though, have not relinquished me. Another title I inherited when my father, Emperor Karl I, died was a perhaps peculiar one from the contemporary point of view—King of Jerusalem. It didn't occur to me to relinquish it, any more than the title Emperor of Mexico. Both had been mute for a long time. However, the King of Jerusalem appellation has been revived by a religious council, Jerusalem's ultra-Orthodox Jewish rabbinate, or at least it is a candidate for recognition by the United Nations. It originated during the Crusades and was probably established by a pope of those times. In any event, it had the church's blessing, a blessing never revoked. That is why, gentlemen, you are here. I have brought along my nephew. Please, Joshua, introduce yourself."

Joshua wondered whether his uncle's testing him would ever stop. He hadn't been told how he would be involved in the King of Jerusalem matter, or explicitly that he was a fully acknowledged family member of the House of Habsburg. He had to wing it. "My name is Joshua Habsburg Heine, a nephew as you have heard. My father was a younger brother of His Highness. However, I was raised in the United States and use the internationalized name Haburghe. I have dual citizenship, Austria's and the USA's, and work in New York as a translator for the United Nations and as a freelance arts writer. How my uncle wants to involve me in the Jerusalem matter I can only conjecture. It may have something to do with my work as translator."

"You look as if you are still in your 20s, early 30s at most. Are you married?" wondered one of the elderly clerics.

Joshua nodded yes, then no and followed it up with "I am 32 and unmarried."

"Age and matrimony are irrelevant for what I have in mind," interjected His Highness, "but something else about Joshua is not. He tells me he is an atheist, though a tolerant one."

The churchmen seemed to ignore this further information about Joshua and began to introduce themselves—names, positions, and nationalities if not Austrian. It appeared to be approximately in order of age that they spoke, and that rather corresponded with rank. The young one's turn came last, of course. He was Brother Sestius, priest and friar, tonsured and cassocked, his eyes were big, dark disks. Usually opaque, they sometimes glowed suddenly like coals in a not-yet-doused fire.

The clerical roll call was too much for Joshua to take in totally yet also too protracted for him to have a clue as to exactly how each of these churchmen counted in the hierarchy. From their presences and relaxed behaviors toward each other, he suspected that they belonged to a clique, one that approved of the clergy's political involvement in the world.

Following the introductions, His Highness again had the first word. "I owe you an explanation of my nephew's presence, and I owe it to him. I am not inclined to refuse the request to become the temporary ruler, more correctly the temporal administrator of Jerusalem's nonconformist Jews, and to be the buffer between them and the Israelis, the Palestinians, and the Christians there. But as you are aware, I am much involved with European unification right now. It is neither seemly nor practical to act as both King of Jerusalem and as European citizen, as Dr. Habsburg. What I want to do is to delegate the Jerusalem obligation to a close and suitable kinsman. The optimal candidate for this task is Joshua. First of all, delegation to a family member is an old and sanctioned imperial and royal privilege even if it needs the pope's consent. Although there are numerous men in my family, they are either too young or too old or too involved in tasks from which they can't be extricated. Joshua is able and, I think, available. Also, he has valuable attributes that distinguish none of the others. He is a trained diplomat and translator. He has studied Hebrew, Arabic, even some Aramaic and knows English and German. In case Yiddish and Ladino are required, I think he could pick those up. Last but not least, I think there is a thoughtful, affirmative air about him. He would cut an apt figure as the acting King of Jerusalem. Joshua, would you accept such an assignment?"

Joshua was sitting up in his straight-backed chair. His focus shifted from his uncle's features to the landscape that lay behind, the living tapestry outside the windows. He was having to improvise what amounted to a campaign talk in the guise of an acceptance speech, compose it as he went along, and deliver it on an empty stomach too. He hadn't had breakfast before leaving Vienna, and lunch would be later. Facing serious men, some stern and noncommittal, others wary, he thought it would help if, mentally, he addressed a single individual. He picked Brother Sestius. "Gentlemen, it is ostensibly on vacation from my work and life in America that I came to Europe. Not that I was tired and in need of rest. Far from it, my experiences in New York have been exciting, stimulating, even satisfying in temporary ways. But how much did they count? In the great UN undertaking to achieve global peace, I was engaged in trivial tasks and felt a craving to contribute something more. It occurred to me that becoming actively a part of the Habsburg family, part of a tradition of political service, might be the way to accomplish something of significance. Not that I knew what needed to be done. I had no idea in general or specifically that a request had come to the UN concerning Jerusalem. That request, though, is an opportunity. The person who helps the ultra-orthodox Jews manage their practical relations with their Israeli, Palestinian, and Christian neighbors could become a catalyst for a broader, a more comprehensive peace among the factions there. I would consider it an honor to be of help in this, even if only as translator. We translators at the UN have been trained to be diplomats too, but stationed in New York, there's not much opportunity to put that into practice. Jerusalem seems a chance to serve."

Of course there were questions for Joshua. He explained that he was between assignments at the UN and would not be abandoning unfinished tasks. He went into some detail about the languages he had studied and where. One of the churchmen did ask Joshua about his atheism, and Joshua explained it as he had to His Highness during their first meeting. The churchman dug further, "You say that if there is a God, the knowledge of him must be intuitive, that it must arise from inside your being and not be learned from an outside authority, not from another human being. You insist that there must be what we call the God within, but you have been unable to find him. Perhaps, though, you have never been close enough to another, paid enough attention to someone else, learned from another, absorbed from one who has faith in the knowledge of God's existence. Learning and love go together. Have you ever been in love?"

"I grew up orphaned from an early age, so did not know parental love. I have no siblings. Friendships, yes, I've had close ones and affairs. Love? As stated earlier, I am single."

"Let's not turn this into a confessional," interrupted one of the elders. "We are here to advise Dr. Habsburg whether he should act on his church-given title, King of Jerusalem, and if yes, whether he should do so himself or delegate the duties to his nephew. First things first: does it benefit or harm our church to have a locally active lay representative in Jerusalem at this time?"

The discussion that ensued was as finely divided as a fugue. Five voices stated the major themes, with the seven others joining in either pro or con. Nothing could be done about the rabbinate's request. It had been made to the UN and officially forwarded as "information" to His Highness. Although he had not yet granted or denied the request to assume the temporal ruler role and the request hadn't so far been commented on by the press, for these things to happen was merely a matter of time. The consensus that emerged among the churchmen coincided with Otto's inclination. It would not do to have the heir to the King of Jerusalem title respond with an outright no. Was there, though, a third way, one which avoided throwing a spotlight on the church's role in maintaining old rights and still intervening in politics? Delegating the Jerusalem function to a nephew would not only free His Highness to act in European affairs but would diminish the public's interest and the press's scrutiny. Joshua seemed to possess the quali-fying skills yet, blessedly, was unknown to the world and would attract less attention than His Highness. That he came from a loyal Roman Catholic family mitigated his personal atheism—at least somewhat. And, just to be sure that the church was kept in the loop, he would be given a clerical advisor.

Brother Sestius, alone among the twelve, remained worried. "Your full last name is Habsburg Heine. Is the Heine from your mother's family, and is it a Jewish family? If so, the Jews would consider you a Jew and ineligible to function as King of Jerusalem."

His Highness again intervened. "Joshua's paternal family obtained the title King of Jerusalem from the Roman Catholic Church and is a traditional Christian family. That's all that matters. His name is not yet in the legal list of family members because we discovered him only recently. It will now take its place there and be entered as simply Joshua Habsburg. Besides, didn't Heinrich Heine, that family's most famous member, convert to Christianity over a century ago?"

It was agreed that His Highness had the church's consent to proceed. Brother Sestius would be sent to Jerusalem to keep an eye on Joshua and serve as the Vatican's emissary to the Holy City's temporal king. All got up from their chairs to stretch. Individually, the churchmen approached His Highness and Joshua with a blessing or good luck wish. Some then paced in the room, hands clasped behind the back or arms folded in front. Others conversed or went to the windows to take in the Danube view. One of the clerics, apparently a resident here at the former abbey, had gone to inform the concierge that lunch could be served, and soon a group of young, aproned women entered into the roomful of men. The first two carried a silky linen cloth in yellow and gray that they unfolded and spread, covering the vast expanse of the tabletop. Others had baskets with plates, cups, drinking glasses, silver utensils, and napkins matching the table cloth. They accomplished setting up for the diners with the precision of a corps de ballet and exited a pair at a time. Joshua couldn't help noting the plates and cups—they were antique Augarten porcelain.

Conversation during the meal centered on the Middle East more than on church matters. Those who spoke the most mentioned Muslim militancy, Soviet Jews managing to exit for Israel, Palestinian versus Jewish enclaves in the West Bank and Gaza, Jordan's and Egypt's stances, different faiths negotiating the time sharing or partitioning of religious sites. The Middle East was a cauldron. Joshua and Brother Sestius were advised to exchange contact information in order to keep abreast of each other's plans to move to Jerusalem. Having finished eating, the two were shown into a small adjoining chamber, equipped as a study. There were pads of paper, sharpened pencils, ballpoint pens on a shelf. As they sat down at a small table, Joshua sensed a wariness in Sestius. Indeed, the friar's first words challenged. "You are homosexual, aren't you? It doesn't matter, or rather it matters no more to me than your being an atheist and Jew, but I want to know with what I'll have to deal."

"And I will have to deal with a celibate. I consider celibacy a crime against nature."

"Crimes and sins are easy to commit. Celibacy is difficult, yet I've managed. Homosexuality is a weakness, and giving into it, as I suspect you do since you mentioned having affairs, makes you not just a criminal in the eyes of the law and a sinner in the Bible's judgment but a poor candidate for being King of Jerusalem. You think you are going to be a peacemaker, but as soon as the warring factions sniff out your flaw, you will become a marked victim. They will try to entrap you, blackmail you, and if that doesn't work, will ridicule you. Look at how compromised Dag Hammarskjöld became. My colleagues here don't realize how hard an assignment they've given me, but it is my duty to cope."

"So, I am to be the cross you'll have to bear. Be that as it may, for me what comes first is that I too want to serve. I will not abuse my kingly status frivolously to copulate. Since I abhor celibacy, perhaps the safest sex for me would be to try to seduce you." Joshua looked for a sign in Sestius's eyes—anger, revulsion, amusement, or desire—but finding nothing, he continued, "There's no telling when the UN will act on this Jerusalem situation although His Highness seems to have ways of greasing the bureaucratic wheels. He must have made his mind up about me, yet still insists that I meet his close friends and pass their scrutiny. So far, they haven't been easy to assemble. Then there is the practical matter of my apartment and belongings in New York. Also, I wanted to pay a short visit to Salonika, where I was born but left too early to remember."

"You could stop in Salonika on the way to Jerusalem. I too have things to do beforehand. The Vatican's approval is guaranteed given the group of my colleagues who are here. However, I must also ask my order's permission to relocate." The consultation between Joshua and Sestius concluded in a businesslike manner. When they returned to the big room next door, goodbyes were already underway. Joshua and His Highness were the first to leave Duernstein. Looking back from the Danube ferry, Joshua wished there had been time to climb that church tower.

Chapter Twenty Two

Blue Evening

Back in Vienna that evening, Joshua allowed himself to feel tired. He had dropped His Highness off at the Imperial, returned the car, and instead of going out on the town, taken the U-Bahn to the Second District and his hotel. Two letters were waiting. One was from Switzerland, according to its stamp, and the other had been posted locally. In his room, he undressed, threw himself onto the bed, and opened the Swiss letter first.

As expected, it was Heinz who had written. He was working in Zurich, and rehearsals were going well. Obliged to make an unexpected run to Vienna, it had been just for the day, and he had tried unsuccessfully to find Joshua at his hotel. He'd left no message because he'd be on his way back to Zurich by the time Joshua would have gotten it. Now, finally in a small sublet, he gave its address and phone number. By the way, Herby had stopped in for a few days and gotten underfoot, but was gone again. Did Josh think he could hop over to Zurich for a day or two?

The other letter, more a note, was from someone he did not know, a Josef Heine. Would Joshua please contact him and do so soon because he might not be in Vienna very long? He was staying at the Hotel Nordbahnhof and had gotten Joshua's whereabouts circuitously from the lawyer handling the Heine Bank restitution case. Joshua remembered the countess mentioning that his mother's inheritance might finally be coming through. He was vaguely aware of his mother having had such a cousin but didn't think the man was still alive. What really interested Joshua was, at last, meeting one of his maternal relatives.

Since it wasn't late, Joshua phoned and was connected to Herr Heine's room. The voice that answered was mellow, very evenly paced yet colorfully accented. Its German substance was spiced by intonations from several lands. That this man must be a wanderer is what Joshua's linguistics training suggested. He could be in his 60s, and the longer they spoke, the more this cousin evinced a comfortable curiosity about Joshua. They agreed to meet for *Gabelfruehstueck*—fork breakfast—midmorning the next day when Joshua would pick him up at Hotel Nordbahnhof.

After they had hung up, Joshua felt utterly exhausted. Responding to Heinz would have to wait, although he kept wondering whether Herby had been along for that day in Vienna and if it had indeed been them he spotted at the Hermesbad. Images of tangled bodies in the steaming sauna slipped from Joshua's waking thoughts into his dreams. They intertwined with Sestius's noncommittal features during their confrontation and the occasional glow that at first introduction had flared in the unconsumed coals that were the young friar's eyes. Waking briefly in the middle of the night, Joshua switched off the light he had forgotten about earlier.

Chapter Twenty Three

A Pencil Drawing

The Hotel Nordbahnhof was situated at the *etoile* end of the Praterstrasse, not far from where Joshua was staying. He had passed it often and seen its brochure, which boasted that the film composer Max Steiner had been born in this building in 1888 and that the Polish playwright Stanislaw Wyspianski resided there in 1904 during a visit to Vienna. It was a respectable businessman's hotel, not at all luxurious, but the thought that he couldn't have afforded it for so lengthy a stay as his current one brought a wry wrinkle to his face—to be precise, the Habsburg smile sat a few moments at the right side of his mouth. It broadened to a very open and welcoming expression when he saw a man, presumably Josef Heine, coming toward him out of the hotel's swinging wood and glass doors.

Herr Heine was moderately tall, broad but not bulky, dressed in unostentatious good taste for a casual midmorning walk, and he carried a large leather portfolio. His eyes darted about with interest in and wonder at the world. Although a suitable café Konditorei adjoined the hotel, he suggested they walk into the Prater and find a place there because, after their getting acquainted talk, he wanted to stay a while to finish a sketch he had begun of the park's great alley of chestnut trees. They ended up at an outdoor table of the same establishment at which Joshua and His Highness had dined and ordered coffee, two big brown ones (coffee with warm milk), and a *Kipfel* (croissant), which came with butter, strawberry jam, and—as always in Vienna—with a glass of the city's crisp Alpine water.

Josef was a first cousin of Joshua's mother. Their fathers had been brothers; both were bankers but had operated in different parts of the world. Joshua's grandfather had focused on Europe, whereas South

America had been his younger sibling's realm. There was overlap in Africa, where they shared a few experimental interests. "I wanted to be a painter, but my father wouldn't permit it other than as a hobby," said Josef. "Probably I studied more than if I'd become an artist full time. I would have been impatient to break away and start on my own. My father sent me to apprentice manage at all our branch banks from Patagonia to Panama. Wherever I was, I'd seek out painters, print makers, draftsmen, even sculptors who weren't averse to giving lessons. I tried all forms. My favorite, though, is drawing. For someone on the move, which I still am, it's the most practical. You don't need a studio or complicated equipment, just paper, a few pencils, and a sharpener. Drawings needn't set or dry. One can pack them up in no time."

Breaking off his narrative to sip from the still steaming cup in front of him and tear a bite-sized portion from the neatly separable piece of pastry on his plate, Josef was taking a pause, and Joshua understood that his cousin hadn't yet finished talking. What he still had to say concerned the remaining Heine clan. It had shriveled during the middle decades of the 20th century, not solely, not directly due to dictatorships and war, but circumstances just weren't right for replenishing the family. "I have a wife and daughter, and a sister who has a daughter. That's all. They live in Rio and are all involved in running the family's concerns, which—unlike the family—have grown. If, as now seems likely, there is restitution of what the European Heine bank had prior to Hitler, there will be further expansion. It would involve you. Tell me, though, who you are—who you want to become!"

The bare contours of Joshua's life were known to Josef, but he was curious about what sort of person this North American "Heine" might turn out to be. Joshua highlighted his urge to do more than work at world peace in a minor way and to do more than dabble in the New York arts scene. Josef's inquisitiveness was palpable as he asked for additional details and probed Joshua about his writing, yet he wasn't testing Joshua. He seemed ready to accept any sort of character as long as it had substance. Still, Joshua hid his personal life insofar as he was leaving it unmentioned.

"I haven't your ambition to matter, to contribute. I'm at peace being a businessman banker and doing drawings during my spare time. Perhaps your willingness to take on the Habsburg assignment will enable you to achieve your goal of serving humanity. I wish you good luck. The money that may come to you with the Heine restitution can only help, since your current finances undoubtedly aren't ample and even Otto von Habsburg isn't flush. Of course, you'll have decisions to make. We must be in touch!"

They finished their fork breakfast, and Josef, as the older and richer relative, insisted on paying the modest bill. Joshua then asked whether he could watch Josef sketch—just for a short while. Josef gave his consent, and they left the establishment to walk up the Prater's chief allee to the bench that gave the drawing its perspective. Sitting down and removing his jacket, Josef folded it neatly, placed it on the bench to his left, and opened the portfolio, which he had positioned to his right. Joshua, standing behind the bench, was looking at a drawing of the view before them. It had been made with colored pencils. The tones on the paper were as intense as those of the three-dimensional scene Josef had used as model. Could this have been achieved with pencils alone and not been aided by some sort of wet pigment? Joshua wondered whether Josef licked his pencils before applying them to the paper. The pad had been held still, but now Josef began shifting it to catch light at different angles. When the reflection was strongest, it almost seemed that the drawing had been made by striking pencils on the paper as if they were matches—to ignite a glow. The colors burned in afterimage even when Joshua closed his eyes. When he opened them again, he noticed the draftsmanship. Contours were remarkably refined; foreshortenings accumulated into a linearity that led the eye to an urgent vanishing point—beyond which hovered a mystery, a puzzle hidden beneath the horizon. Joshua looked away, raised his eyes, and beheld the actual scene. When he focused on the drawing again, he tried to place it as art. He couldn't guess its niche, its period. There weren't any of the familiar signposts of style, and it lay on the artist's lap so real but an anomaly, an artifact unrelated to history.

"You could have been a full-time artist. Thank you for giving me a glimpse."

Josef was already working at the unfinished upper-right corner of the drawing. "If you like it, I'll send it to you when it is done. I'll finish it today, the day of our meeting, and date it as such." It was the 14th of September 1977.

Chapter Twenty Four

A Farewell Embrace

The gathering of friends His Highness hoped for proved impossible to arrange. No matter how often Frl. Andrea combed calendars for an available day, there was not one in common for even a representative minority of the group. These were busy people, these men and one woman, especially now that it was autumn. "Two of them you've met anyway," His Highness remarked to Joshua.

"Was one of them the elder priest who did not want to turn the session at Duernstein into a confessional? I thought I detected sympathy, affection between him and you."

His Highness nodded.

"But who is the other?"

"Your cousin, Josef Heine."

Joshua was astonished. Nothing about this Habsburg-Heine point of contact had ever been mentioned to him before. "An interesting man, I suspect, although we met just once."

"He wasn't able to contact you before he had to depart Vienna, but he left something for you in my care," His Highness said. They were sitting in His Highness's suite at the Imperial, and from a cupboard, His Highness withdrew a large flat package. "It is the drawing he promised you. May I ask you to look inside? I'm an admirer of Josef's art."

Joshua too was curious to see the finished work. He opened the paper wrapping carefully and from inside it pulled out two large sketch pad sheets that had been placed back to back between two pieces of cardboard. On one sheet was the drawing of the Prater's main allée. It throbbed, colorfully. Although formally finished, it yet left room in the imagination for additions: perhaps a rider on horseback would appear on the bridle path stretching into the distance, or people would walk along the roadway or cross paths or seat themselves on a bench. The scene seemed inclined to becoming inhabited. Was it that shadows of still absent objects and bodies were already being cast in anticipation of their arrival?

On the other sheet was a portrait sketch of a woman, dated 2 June 1947. She had piercing eyes, yet much of the drawing seemed faded, or had the paper aged? It made her coloration seem pale, sickly. The only other thing depicted was a chair in which the woman sat. It wasn't fully realized, just indicated, yet it looked substantial. Showing the woman's tentative health had been intentional. Joshua identified her as his mother.

"How like Josef. He doesn't keep what he draws. He may have been saving your late mother's portrait for you until you had grown up. I remember our families being at the same Riviera resort one summer long ago. He would make a sand sculpture almost every day for the children's amusement. They were amazingly sensual forms that craved permanence, that yearned for life, but every night the tide would erode them and the waves would wash them away. He didn't seem to mind, nor would he permit anyone to photograph them. Their precarious existence was part of their appeal."

Joshua had taken a deep breath at the sight of the portrait showing his mother inclining to death, yet he would not react more intensely until he was by himself. His Highness had noticed the breath but, respecting Joshua's privacy, went on to discuss immediate plans and preparations for Jerusalem. The Vatican had been quick to respond. It approved of delegating the King of Jerusalem title to His Highness's nephew and had already appointed Brother Sestius as its ambassador to his court. The rabbis who had made the request weren't thrilled having a substitute for His Highness and especially not one so young, but weren't saying no. They were furnishing a house for their new temporal and perhaps temporary ruler. Palatial it wasn't yet was nothing to be ashamed of. Opening on two sides into a substantial garden and surrounded by a high wall, it also boasted a sheltered roof deck with fine views of the surrounding so-called mountains—hills really.

In contrast to the religious bodies, the political ones hadn't yet consented. However, His Highness felt sure that Israel's government would. The UN's recognition was being delayed by squabbles among the Arab states, some of which felt that sanctioning even a non-Israeli Jewish enclave in Jerusalem would set a bad precedent.

His Highness's stay in Vienna was coming to an end. He was about to go home to Germany. He advised Joshua to undertake his Salonika visit while waiting for the UN's decision. "Later, you'll likely not have the time." There would be a small gathering for family goodbyes to His Highness, which would serve too to simplify Joshua's leave-taking. As their last private conversation came to an end, His Highness embraced his nephew.

Frl. Andrea, before departing with His Highness, helped Joshua arrange his Salonika sojourn. They booked his trip there and his hotel, but not a return—in case he would have to proceed directly to Jerusalem. Actually, it was from Brother Sestius that they learned about the trains he could take. Railways were the young friar's one worldly passion. He collected schedules, perhaps memorized many routes and connections, not just for Europe but around the globe. For Joshua's starting out, he recommended the train that had already brought him from Zurich to Vienna. The *Vienna Waltzes* was an alternative to the *Orient Express*, had bathrooms and showers plus the advantage for Joshua of covering more of the track east from Vienna in daylight. It was terrain he didn't know. He would have to change trains twice en route to Salonika, once in Budapest, and then after Bucharest, at the border of Bulgaria, Turkey, and Greece. Briefly, he wondered about going in the opposite direction first, to visit Heinz in Zurich, but he rejected that option. It would distract. Joshua needed to be alone.

Chapter Twenty Five

Salonika Sojourn

The farther east the rails took Joshua from Vienna, the less civilized, the wilder the landscape and villages became. He recalled—was it Metternich's quip?—that the Orient starts right after one crosses Vienna's Ringstrasse on the road to Budapest. His last train wasn't an express but a Greek local that took him to his destination with lots of stops, yet all in all it was a short ride.

Salonika turned out to be a typical Mediterranean port town—many white buildings of fairly recent design. After being cooped up so much of the time since departing Vienna, he needed to stretch his legs. So Joshua checked into his hotel and headed out to explore. His first impression, though, remained. Behind the shoreline and beyond Aristotelus Square, Salonika was a predictable place. Perhaps when he went to the wooded mountains behind the city, where the guerillas had hidden and he had been born, he'd find enchantment. Frl. Andrea had given him the name and contact information of one of his parents' cohorts who was still alive and had stayed in Salonika. Her name was Ruth, and she lived in an elder-care residence for the city's few remaining Jews. When Joshua phoned, she invited him to come and sit with her on her room's shaded balcony and talk. She served tea and pointed out the harbor sights that were to be had from her balcony and also the tops of the inland mountains. It was the woman's face, though, that fascinated Joshua. With its leathery skin and the unyielding gaze of her eyes, it was close to being a mask. Ruth's voice, though, was warm and vibrant as she told of the changes she had seen Salonika submit to during her life. The city had been practically

Jewish prior to World War II, but so many of her co-religionists had been deported to camps by the Nazi occupation forces. A minority, mostly leftists, had joined the bands of resistance fighters in the mountains. After the war, most Jews who had not been killed in the camps or had survived in the mountains, immigrated to Israel. The ones who remained had done so for individual, usually very personal reasons. She did not explain what had caused her to stay. Salonika, however, was no longer the same. It had become quite another town—ethnically, architecturally, temperamentally, but disconcertingly at the same site between mountains and sea as the one in which she had spent her youth.

Ruth had been close to Joshua's mother and attended both ceremonies, the Jewish and the Greek Orthodox one, that married his parents. "Under the circumstances, we were very proud that we could arrange for not just one but two." To get up into the mountains where that had taken place and where Joshua had been born, she recommended hiring a car and driver. "If I'm not up to coming with you, I'll write directions for the driver and explanations for you."

It wasn't a long drive. The former sharp demarcation between city and countryside had been erased. Ruth's note to Joshua mentioned that the urban sprawl he would encounter had originated some time after the war. When the car did emerge into fields and farmland, the road began to ascend steeply. Soon stretches of forest more than meadows dominated the scene. The guerillas had encamped where the tree canopies were thickest, so they couldn't easily be spotted from rocky outlooks or from the air. They kept their campsites small and scattered, moving them often. However, Ruth remembered where Joshua had been delivered from his mother's womb. It was at the top perimeter of a great grove known since antiquity as Hermes's Woods and made of a mix of fir trees and leaf trees. An old barn, half hidden by the trees, was the only building within miles. The guerillas left it unused except for the delivery and the mother and infant's first night. It was a distance from the nearest road, and Joshua took the walk by himself, leaving the driver behind. He found a new barn, but it was built on old foundations. The scene was rustic enough, yet didn't particularly speak to him. His imagination balked at conjuring up his mother or a younger Ruth. He peered through the crack between barn door and doorframe, but it was too dim inside the structure to see much, and the door latch wouldn't budge. Outside, Joshua circled the barn and then sat down on a rock and continued trying to see things in a memorable light until he gave up and turned his back on the place in order to return to the car.

Joshua's hotel room was booked for a week. He visited Ruth again and, too, was able to lure her out for a meal on a day when she felt well enough to dress up and walk in high heels. The stylish way she wore her hair on this occasion and the up-to-date cut of her jacket and dress were a surprise. Joshua offered Ruth his arm and being escorted affected her like the fountain of youth.

The time he had on his hands was spent taking long walks through urban and suburban Salonika. Usually at the start of these forays, he paid close attention to civic details—the sorts of shops, the differences among those of the same type, the heights of buildings, the street space left for flowers and greenery, variations in pavement materials and patterns. Soon, though, his thoughts slipped to his own situation. Joshua became almost oblivious to his whereabouts while he juggled his impressions of Otto Habsburg's and Josef Heine's lives. To be involved with the world or not to be? Had he made his choice already? Was it too late to return to being a translator and writer, try to be as good as possible in those roles and find satisfaction in minding his own garden? Otto could never have escaped his lot. Joshua was still, legally, an orphan and could do what he wanted without hurting anyone else. Although Otto would find it inconvenient to replace him, that shouldn't be impossible given the extent of the family.

On one of his walks, Joshua wondered about the value of writing not about life, or a life, directly but about the arts. Was there a gulf between journalistic criticism, with its tight deadlines and rationed space, and the old Oriental habit of taking a lifetime to look at a single work of art and then sum up one's response in a haiku that desecrated vacant space on the very same piece of parchment as the art work? That reportage and reviewing could be poetry had been proven by Edwin Denby, Claudia Cassidy, Carl Van Vechten, and Heinrich Heine. The haiku writers also had to be skilled calligraphers. Was commentary of either sort like a beam of light that could give an artifact added dimension and a little of life's complexity, or was it just vanity? Joshua missed writing. To occupy his evenings in Salonika, he started telling Ruth's tale. He knew the facts, he guessed her reasons. After buying a new notebook and a smoother, sharper pen, he wondered whether the first words he'd put down would be English or German.

Toward the end of the week, letters arrived. The Countess Zdenka was back in Vienna and wondering whether there would be a chance to see him. Frl. Andrea wrote she was arranging his flight from Salonika to Tel Aviv. Did he need funds? He would be met at Tel Aviv Airport by a member of the Jerusalem rabbinate, and they'd proceed by car. Yes, it appeared that the Arab states had given their consent!

A letter from Heinz had been forwarded by Joshua's Vienna hotel. The revival of the dance work had been a success. Too bad that Josh couldn't have come to see it, but there would be another chance. Zurich now wanted him to mount a triple bill—the revival, the piece recently choreographed in New York, and something new. He had said yes but felt the need for a holiday first. Where was Joshua going to be?

Chapter Twenty Six

King House

Two people waited for Joshua at Tel Aviv Airport. He had expected one—a representative of the ultra-Orthodox rabbinate, of the Haredim, the Jews who would not acknowledge Israel as a state. This man introduced himself to Joshua as Rabbi Aaron ben Ai. The other, an Israeli government official, got Joshua through passport control and immigration. Otherwise the procedure would have taken forever because of security precautions. The Israeli representative's name was Uri Lichtenfels. Aaron and Uri, although opposed, conversed politely with one another. Was it because they had become habituated to what was a long-standing conflict or out of consideration for the newly arrived Joshua? They avoided issues, preferring to keep to mundane matters such as Joshua's schedule for the next couple of days. Aaron had assumed that Joshua was coming from New York and would need more than a night to adjust his biological clock. Uri knew better and offered to show Joshua around Jerusalem during the city's institutionalized Friday to Sunday weekend that was coming up. The driver of the car taking them to Jerusalem, Benjamin, offered his services for the driving that would be needed to sightsee. He was in his 20s, this Benjamin, and sported a bright red beard and matching locks yet wasn't dressed in the black-and-white, dingily formal Haredi way, so Joshua couldn't quite place him. Other than make his offer, the driver didn't participate in the talk but did seem to be listening intently.

The landscape through which they passed was still waiting for autumn rains. There were rocky hills, frugal trees, sandy slopes with parched patches of grass. As the car left the highway and entered Jerusalem, the initial image of the eternal city that established itself in Joshua's mind was that of a temporary permanence—apartment buildings of recent design but not built to last, which seemed to provide certain amenities such as balconies, window ledges with flower boxes, and television antennae neatly corralled on rooftops. A few older, smaller, durable houses, some with red-tiled roofs, were scattered about between the concrete housing blocks. Further in, Jerusalem became a city of stone. It was harder to guess the age of structures, but some seemed venerable. Jerusalem rock had a characteristic tint: the big dose of daylight in it was marked by dark clusters that hovered like storm clouds in a golden firmament .Yet at a distance, at acute angles, the stone's cratered surface was suffused by a blush.

They had to stop to refuel, an operation that fascinated Aaron. He was as curious as a little boy might have been, and afterward Joshua couldn't help but think of the rabbi as someone from a long-ago time. Soon after, they drew up at a four-story house at the corner of a small square and a narrow side street. This was to be Joshua's home, the King of Jerusalem's abode. It didn't at all seem palatial in the Schoenbrunn sense. It did, because of the solidity of its building blocks, its height and that of the adjoining wall surrounding what must have been a very compact garden, have something of the fortified look of a miniature castle. The house had no direct entrance from the square or the street. There was just one gate in the garden wall. It was solid, of dark wood, so one could not see inside. Aaron rang the bell once, waited, and then rang a second time. Receiving no response from inside, he reached into his briefcase, drew out a sizeable key and handed it to Joshua. "It is right that you, as new resident and soon to be ruler, should unlock the door." Joshua did, and the door swung to the inside, into a passageway through what proved to be a very thick wall to a second door. That also had to be unlocked. It opened into the garden. There were just a couple of steps to the house door. Joshua inserted the key and turned it a third time. Benjamin had come up with Joshua's single suitcase and went off to repark the car. The three others entered.

Suddenly there were four. From out of the shadows of the great room on the ground floor stepped a lad. He approached Aaron, but his eyes lit up as he beheld Joshua standing there with his suitcase. "This is your servant, Afsan," Aaron explained to Joshua, "The budget can afford only one full-time staff member. There will be others who come in for different domestic and secretarial tasks, but Afsan is quartered here, and the two of you will be the permanent residents of what we've been calling the king's house. Afsan is from a Palestinian Christian family but also has fluent command of English and Hebrew." Belatedly, Aaron chided Afsan, "Where have you been? We rang twice and then let ourselves in."

Any explanation was precluded by Joshua reaching out to shake hands with Afsan, who then took the suitcase. With a nod, or more a bow, he withdrew with it, presumably to deposit the baggage in the master bedroom.

Joshua was to meet the rest of the rabbinate on Monday, here in the great room. Tomorrow, Friday, Aaron and Uri would begin showing Joshua around Jerusalem. Benjamin hadn't yet returned—it wasn't always easy to find secure parking in the older parts of the city—but undoubtedly he'd be available to do driving. They would also do more than a bit of walking. After giving Joshua their phone numbers and that of his own house, Aaron and Uri departed, and Afsan conducted Joshua to his room. It was on the top floor, under the roof garden, a corner room with views of the Old City and Mount Scopus. Joshua didn't feel like unpacking and asked to be shown the house. Counting the roof garden and the cellar, there were actually six levels. None of the rooms was as yet fully furnished, but all had recently been plastered, painted, and wood-stained, so there was a reborn air in the old structure.

While Afsan was complaining how much stair climbing he had to do, the bell rang. It was Benjamin returning. Joshua asked Afsan to make tea for the three of them, and as the two young men watched the lad's near ceremonial procedure, Joshua began questioning Benjamin about his background. He was surprised to hear Benjamin say he had American ancestry and dual citizenship—American and Israeli, which he didn't think was quite legal in the USA. Back in the 19th century, Benjamin's white, Midwestern great-grandparents had belonged to a fundamentalist Protestant sect. Their pastor was convinced that Christ's second coming was imminent. The entire congregation, practically, decided to await the event in Jerusalem, where the Lord would first appear. They had sold all their nontransportables and set up a small commune in the holy city. As time went on and their money began to disappear, they realized they had miscalculated by a few years, centuries, or millennia and would have to earn their keep in Jerusalem. Mostly, they went into the hotel business, and did so quite successfully. There was a lack of middle-class hotels of Western caliber not only in Jerusalem but throughout the Middle East. In fact, tourism from America and Europe had been held back until the founding of this enterprise that catered to the need. The descendants of the original commune kept close, intermarried much, or went back to the Middle West for spouses. Only his generation, now in its twenties, was beginning to drift. Benjamin himself was not a believer. He also had tried the Haredi stance, hence the beard and locks, and hadn't even balked at circumcision. Nevertheless, he ended up an atheist. His rebellion having started when he was fairly young, the commune had never bothered giving Benjamin the trip to America that had become standard for all of its young men and women in good standing. He'd never been. Nor had the commune seen fit to find him a job in its enterprises. He was on his own, so he tried being a driver, mostly for the Haredim. It was working out. Joshua listened to the story and wondered what else Benjamin would try.

The sun had set by the time Benjamin left, and although Joshua wanted to go out by himself, map in hand, Afsan dissuaded him. The lad made them supper, a modestly good Near Eastern one which they ate in Joshua's second private room—a sitting-room study. Joshua asked him about the community into which he had been born, but, despite talking a lot, he managed to say little. After doing the dishes, Afsan asked whether it would be all right for him to go out to visit his family. He'd be back in his room, behind the great room, well before midnight. Joshua gave him leave and received the assurance that all three doors would be securely locked when Afsan left and when he returned. Joshua went to unpack his suitcase and fell asleep alone in the faint light of a crescent moon filtering through gauze curtains onto his bed in his castle.

Three days of sightseeing gave Joshua a crash course in Jerusalem, its statistics, and its lore. Uri and Aaron were his guides, except on Saturday when the observant Aaron absented himself. Benjamin helped the touring about too, not just as driver but as informant concerning things that impinged less on the older men's awareness. Jerusalem essentially was a beehive city, partitioned by race, religion, nationality, and generation. Yet there were also connections among the distinct enclaves, tentative and semi-subversive umbilici being formed, dissolved, and reformed by the youth generation. On Saturday, they had lunch at one of the underground cafes where the clientele tried to forget faith, family, and fatherland; Uri was distinctly older than any other customer, and Joshua almost so. History's icons—the Temple Mount with its mosque and dome, the Old City's residential quarters, the Wailing Wall, the Stations of the Cross—impressed themselves on Joshua's retina. He had to recalibrate his sense of height to see Jerusalem's hills as mountains, but by the end of the first day, as the sunset ignited a cloud bank above the horizon, he began to see the stubborn beauty of this aged, ageless terrain.

On Saturday night, Afsan, who kept asking to go out in the evenings, slipped up in his family visit excuse, and Joshua was able to persuade the lad to take him along. They cruised along avenues and streets that now were lamp lit and nearly deserted except for the occasional stroller here and there—men whose casual approach betrayed tensions that more than once triggered a rapid retreat. They skirted shadowy alleys in which a single bare light outlined a doorway opening into a seamy, seemingly empty den. Jerusalem was not a city for facile nightlife, but apparently Afsan knew how to negotiate its jeopardies. Managing to make a pickup, he insisted that the man wait for him while he escorted Josh back to King House.

Chapter Twenty Seven

The Rabbinate

The ten men who met in the great room on the ground floor of King House reminded Joshua of the twelve Catholic clerics at Abbey Duernstein, only all of this group were bearded, wore just black and white, and—although not expected to be celibate—each one seemed even more unworldly, more *weltfremd*. The room, provisionally furnished with folding chairs and card tables, was nevertheless festive with its newly painted walls, deeply tinted posts and beams, and the silky cloths of Egyptian cotton with which Afsan had covered the card tables. An older rabbi—he had a thoughtful, long face such as Rembrandt would have wanted to paint and an infant's large, innocent, inquisitive eyes—was the one to whom the others deferred. He took up the word, welcoming Joshua again, although "undoubtedly our brother Aaron welcomed you well at the airport."

Joshua's response was that of a skilled juggler. He acknowledged the welcomes, including his introduction to the sights of the city, as those due a King of Jerusalem. However, as someone who was not yet king and only deputy and designate, he made it clear how honored he felt. He told the rabbinate a little about his previous life but omitted any mention of having been born to a Jewish mother. He emphasized that he had wanted to serve in some capacity, and enumerated his linguistic and diplomatic qualifications for dealing with Jerusalem. That he would become king was beyond his expectations. Joshua concluded his speech with a question about what work was most urgent. What could he do now?

The answer he received from Aaron was that the first and foremost need was a measure to regulate relations with Israel. "They give us our water; we give them our sewage. They direct traffic for us, and we butcher their kosher meat. Yet we do not recognize each other. For us to acknowledge Israel is against our belief. There can be no Jewish state since the Messiah has not yet come! For them to admit to our independence undermines Israel's sovereignty and would set a precedent for the independence not only of the Palestinians but that of all other resident minorities—the Druze, Circassians, Samaritans, Christians of various nationalities like the American enclave of our driver Benjamin's family."

"Practically, how can I complain about my sewage clogging up and my tap water running dry to someone I do not recognize?" The senior rabbi turned his expectant long face from Joshua and looked up at the light pouring in from a high window.

Joshua's ideas were American. "I think we can learn from Thomas Jefferson and those who drafted the constitution of the United States. They had to deal with the red Indians within their borders. Later, America had to accommodate a kingdom, Hawaii, within a democratic assembly of states. The Indian tribes remained independent nations within the USA. Hawaii had inhabitants of varied allegiances to the Hawaiian queen and to American presidents. Give me a lawyer to work with, and we'll solve this diplomatic issue faster than you can turn on the water tap."

Joshua had scored a point, at least until the lawyers, the constitutional authorities, and the theologians would begin to examine the possibility he proposed. It was just as well that the press hadn't picked up on his arrival in Jerusalem or on the nature of his assignment. That would give him time to establish contacts in the diverse communities with which the Haredim had to deal. To forge peace, Joshua had to consider not just Israel and the Haredi Jews but think about all of Jerusalem's factions. It would be more difficult to send feelers out once he was in the limelight, after his coronation—which the Haredim had persuaded the UN and the Vatican should happen before Hanukkah. He didn't look forward to the prospect of kneeling in church. On the other hand, he'd not had the chance to dress up in royal drag since once long ago in a boarding school play.

Although the first conference between the rabbinate and Joshua was over, he sat down with the elder rabbi and with Aaron to set up accounts and map his schedule. Aaron had been appointed to keep the "Kingdom's" accounts and serve as secretary. Already there was a list of those seeking an appointment with Joshua, and the names he recognized were Brother Sestius, Uri Lichtenfels, and Zara Hoffmann. What in the world would Zara from Yorkville, Manhattan, New York, be doing in Jerusalem?

Chapter Twenty Eight

Israel's Appeal

"Keeping appointments is something I'm not about to do," Joshua insisted jokingly, "but I'll consent to giving audiences." Those who called at King House might be asked to seat themselves in the great room on the ground floor where the folding chairs and card tables hadn't yet been replaced by anything more permanent. For the "study," Joshua had in a hurry acquired solid, dark wooden furnishings. The bookcases there stood waiting for his belongings to arrive from New York. On the roof, there was simple garden furniture under an awning, and Afsan had planted flower beds and potted a few not-too-tall trees. Weather permitting, Joshua preferred receiving callers on his roof garden.

The first appointment following the session with the Haredim went to Uri, as representative of modern Israel. Uri was aware of Joshua's suggestion that the Haredim be treated like red Indian tribes in America—as semiautonomous vacuoles within the mother cell. "We'd thought of that too, but have hesitated because it would be costly. The Haredim, like all of today's fundamentalists, want more than merely the freedom to follow their own rules. They can't stand anyone who doesn't. It is an abomination in their eyes to have to confront someone who drives a car on the Sabbath, to witness a person eating sausage on a slice of buttered bread, to see a woman toss her natural head of hair. Moreover, taking offense isn't their own doing, the result of their own decision; instead, it becomes the innocent perpetrator's fault, and the blameless are accused of being offenders. We could build high walls around the neighborhoods the Haredim dominate, turn them into true ghettos, but they will not stay put. They are ever more militant, they insist on going everywhere, and everyone in eye shot must obey their impossible code of behavior."

Uri seemed about to pause, but, at most, he slowed a bit while turning a corner in his tirade. "Every concession Israel makes to its ultra-orthodox requires an analogous measure for the other minorities, not to mention the local Arabs. These—the so-called Palestinians—are more divided than Israel is, more split politically, religiously, by temporality, and especially by class—the wealth gap between rich and poor is enormous. Israel's territory is tiny compared to the spread of Arab lands. The local Arabs claim all of the Jordan's East Bank, parts of the West Bank, practically the totality of Gaza, plus eastern Jordan and beyond. Let's face it: Jordan is a Palestinian state although the UN is deaf, blind, and nasally inert to that truth. To create more independent enclaves in Israel would turn the country into Swiss cheese. It is simply impractical. This is not a rich, ripe region of the world. Resources are scarce, especially potable water. The Arab communities constantly complain that Israel steals their portion of the trickle that is the Jordan, yet they perpetually pollute and otherwise waste their allocation.

"Nor is the Mediterranean's southeast shore a holy land; it is a sink hole, a rotten place to live. And yet it is the only spot on the face of the Earth that by any stretch of the imagination, by any evidence from the past, has an association with the Jews. I know the Arab states have proposed planting a Jewish state somewhere in sub-Saharan Africa or Middle Europe. Ridiculous. Nowhere in the livable world is there uninhabited land. Yet history has proven over and over again that every people should have a land; the need is basic. To be able to breathe the air without begging for that right, to be able to look up into the sky with one's feet planted on inherited ground, to take a few steps in whatever direction one wants and then turn around without having to ask permission—such things are everyone's right. Without them you can't have full human beings."

Uri had exhausted himself. They sat in silence for a few moments, looking out at the city bathed in autumn sunlight and listening to the drone of distant traffic and what seemed the very far off hum of voices. Then

Joshua rang the bell to the kitchen and, in a tone almost as spent as Uri's, concluded, "There you have it. Everyone wants a country of his own. Perhaps we'll have to have something other than monogamy in matters of nationality and territory." Uri responded indirectly. He wanted Joshua to meet Israelis of all stripes—members of old families that had no history of going into diaspora or had returned soon, also the descendants of the first Zionist settlers, immigrants from India and other Asian and African lands, refugees from Communism, American Zionists. As they were making plans to go on visits, a servant appeared—it wasn't Afsan but one of the part-time women—and Joshua asked her to bring them tea—cold, iced tea. The woman wrinkled her brow, and Joshua knew it was because of the ice.

Chapter Twenty Nine

Palestine's Plaints

The two residents of King House were alone together after supper one night when Afsan approached Joshua conspiratorially. At first, Joshua thought the lad wanted his permission to go out cruising or was trying to tempt him into joining in. Instead, he asked whether he might admit a visitor, someone who wished to talk business. It would be a member of the Palestinian community, an individual Afsan could vouch for as safe although affiliated with Fatah—Yasser Arafat's liberation organization. Joshua knew that eventually he would have to seek out Fatah and other Palestinian factions, but already the mountain was coming to him, and he welcomed the opportunity although he foresaw that the climb would be tough—more so than his conversations with the Israeli Jews he had been getting to know due to Uri's mediation. He had spent the previous days listening to talk that both tired and exhilarated him. In all the dark declarations about national exclusivity, there were glints of compromise, of concession, even of cooperation.

Afsan didn't think it wise to telephone the proposed visitor. He left the house and after half an hour returned, accompanied by two individuals— a young, clean shaven, soldierly man and a professorial one who had graying hair, kept gesticulating with gravity whenever he spoke, and on occasion twitched the right corner of his mustache. Both visitors thanked Joshua courteously for being willing to see them on such short notice. Seated in Joshua's study, the young one explained and complained, "We can't always go about like free citizens in our own land. And travel is far from the only restriction. Our way of life is endangered. It revolves around the family, and it is our kinship ties that Israeli measures are countermanding. Land that was ours for millennia is being taken away and given to immigrants from God knows where. We are being disbarred from advantageous professions. The sense of community in our neighborhoods and townships is becoming impossible to maintain. Home is no longer home for us, and not so long ago we were by far the majority. The men of my generation find the situation intolerable. We are dedicating our lives to fight this alien incursion."

The other visitor took off the spectacles he was wearing to hold them, like a lecturer's pointer aimed alternately at his listeners and at himself. And like a conductor with a baton, he wielded his glasses to sharpen a particular phrase or soften the one that followed. "Experience and travel have taught me certain things. There is that which one must accept and there is that which one must oppose. Jerusalem will always be a magnet for those not native to Palestine. It has the misfortune of being the holy city for different faiths. I can live with that. To an extent, I even enjoy it. That is no excuse, though, for disrupting the lives of Palestine's native population. That the Polish Jews were pogrommed, that the Nazis genocided their Jews, that Stalin purged Jews from the Communist Party and exiled them to Siberia are problems that should be rectified in the places where those things occurred—Poland, Germany, and the Soviet Union. The Palestinians have done nothing to deserve the Zionist influx into their country. Herzl himself, who devised Zionism, first proposed a quite different solution to Europe's Jewish problem—mass conversion and integration throughout that continent. Only the churches wouldn't have it. If not Christian baptism, then at least integration as took place in India, but even that isn't happening. That Herzl then proposed Zionism, resettling the world's Jews in Palestine, was an act of desperation, a measure of last resort.

"I work here among the Palestinians as a physician—supposedly an objective, a scientific and humanitarian, an apolitical task. My patients have their problems. The population is prone to dietary difficulties, and, aggravated by smoking among the men, there is little resistance to respiratory infections. I try to both prevent and treat. However, the UN and Israel interfere. They object to some of our routine, traditional procedures. Also, they want me and other local physicians to waste time and resources sleuthing for alien ailments. Palestine is a family society; we don't want and haven't got the West's degeneracies. Clitoral surgery works wonders in some instances to calm women. It reduces the female tendency to hysteria. As for sexually transmitted disease, there is little because prostitution is practically absent, and we haven't any homosexuals among us. Let us alone and we'll be healthier." As the good doctor was delivering himself of his opinions, Afsan entered the room to serve sweet cakes and tea—hot tea since it was nigh time. His eyes carefully avoided Joshua's gaze. The visitors proposed plans for Joshua to meet Palestinian families "at home," and Joshua accepted the offer.

Chapter Thirty

The Vatican's Wishes

Brother Sestius was wearing a cassock of a lighter cloth than when Joshua had seen him in Austria. The material weighed less, was softer, and had been tinted a less intense blue. The way its folds fell suggested that Sestius might have a sexy body. His manner, however, was again severe. He had taken full note of Afsan, and as soon as he and Joshua were alone, he said he felt relieved to see he wouldn't be needed to satisfy Joshua's lust.

"You are right about the boy being available, but satisfy yourself," Joshua replied with a smile. "My bed type he's not."

"The two things we have to discuss are your coronation and the problems I've discovered with the Catholic Church's properties. Sharing our sacred sites here goes way beyond the ecumenicism of Vatican II. On whose terms do we alternate or cohabit? *Primus inter pares;* isn't Rome first among equals?"

"In your Austria, Catholicism has opponents but no real competitors. Here in Jerusalem, there are all the Orthodox Christian churches and their mostly married, more macho priests. Have you become envious?"

"I chose the Roman Catholic priesthood with full knowledge of its obligations, opportunities, and restrictions. Stop heckling me, or you'll spoil this chance we have to establish a truthful kingdom. What you said that day at the abbey about our Jerusalem assignment potentially involving much more than relations between Israel and the ultra-Orthodox Jews is true. Let's, though, proceed peacefully, carefully, one step at a time."

Joshua now felt like going on the attack. "You started our squabble. The day we met you called me a flighty fairy. And again today, you assume I am spending my time here dallying with Afsan. You can't conceive of sexuality being anything more satisfying, more substantial than scratching an itch. Sensual relations refresh not just the body but also the mind. A person can be reborn by the experience of physical love, can be prepared, tempered to tackle the most difficult of tasks."

"Don't preach. Let's be practical and begin to plan the coronation. There is a church here I want to show you. It probably has room enough for all the requisite guests, but also is acoustically apt for the music. I've done some sleuthing, and there actually is music for the King of Jerusalem. It hasn't been performed in centuries, and if word gets out, all the music critics will want to come."

"Will we bring over the Vienna Choir Boys to sing it? In that case, to match their sailor suits, my coronation robe will have to be of blue velvet and white ermine. Seriously, will the December date suit His Highness? He'll have to be here in person to pass the title on."

"Otto von Habsburg is prepared to be here when needed. The Vatican will underwrite the coronation costs. There are, though, two problems— the cooperation of the Orthodox congregations with whom we share the church and security measures. A Habsburg or two, Israeli and UN officials, representatives of other nations, diverse rabbis, and Christian clergy gathered in one spot will be a temptation few terrorists could resist."

"Would inviting the Palestinians and some Sunni and Shia imams make things safer or not?"

Brother Sestius suggested dates for visiting the coronation church and for going to hear a chorus at one of the desert monasteries. Enlisting local singers for the ceremony would be more practical than importing a choir from Europe. Sestius also mentioned a letter he had received from a Zara Hoffmann, apparently one of Joshua's New York acquaintances. Mrs. Hoffmann would be coming to Jerusalem with an NGO, a non-governmental organization, involved in human rights. On her and her group's agenda was a meeting with Joshua in his role as spokesperson for the Haredim. She had heard of Joshua's task from her "contacts" in the Vatican, and to reach him, the Vatican had directed her to Sestius. Confusingly, there was no mention when Zara and her group would arrive.

"What gives her the prerogative to be a player?" Joshua wondered out loud. "Let's not postpone our plans. If we're not at home when Mrs. Hoffmann and her minions come calling, she'll just have to wait."

Chapter Thirty One

Excursion

Overall, the direction of the road leading from Jerusalem to Jericho is down, yet there are serpentines that scale mountainsides, drop into dark gorges, and climb skyward again before descending to 260 meters below sea level. Zigzags of temperature and pressure also make this a treacherous drive because car engines tend to clog and stall or to overheat and boil. Joshua didn't trust his own or Sestius's skills at the wheel, and there was the possibility of having to make repairs, so he arranged for the experienced Benjamin to chauffeur them to the Greek Orthodox monastery reputed to have a notable choir. Of course, Joshua wanted, too, to see the site of the citywall his famous biblical namesake had caused to crack and split asunder. The distance from Jerusalem to the monastery and Jericho wasn't great in terms of kilometers. If they set out early, it would be possible to get back to Jerusalem before the night was too far along. Still, Benjamin advised staying over. There were several possibilities. His familial commune ran a comfortable hotel in Jericho. The monastery they would be visiting had rooms for male visitors. There was also an arts colony in the desert nearby that had guest quarters. Sestius was not eager to stay overnight, but each of the three travelers agreed to pack a small portmanteau just in case.

On the day of the trip, Benjamin picked Joshua up at King House and then Sestius at the Catholic hostel in which he had been given one of the permanent rooms. It was a companionable trio that set out. Joshua was determined not to respond to heckling from Sestius nor to start on that path himself. At the outset, Benjamin did most of the talking.

He had to tell his story to Sestius and expected to hear Sestius's tale in return but was disappointed. One of Sestius's vows was to be reborn, to live in the present and not rummage in the past. He kept it as strictly as his other promises. What caught and held Joshua and Sestius's attention during the drive were the features of a landscape new to them, the surprising variety of color and contour contained in this terrain of eroded rock and stark or stacked and stratified sand. "Were the hermits who withdrew to the desert not sensualists rather than ascetics?" Joshua wondered, and Sestius merely nodded in response.

Their first stop was for the choir at the monastery. Perched precariously on the side of a cliff, the compound's structures were like hands raised skyward in prayer. Sestius had been in touch with the choirmaster, so this was an expected visit. First they were conducted to the midday meal, which was frugal and passed in silence except for the reading beforehand of a prayer. Joshua counted sixty-five resident monks, and there were no other visitors that day than the three. Introductions were noticeably lacking. Following the sitting—which was brought to a close when the monk in charge, presumably the abbot, rang a hand bell—the choirmaster consulted briefly with the visitors. Sestius had brought along a photocopy of the King of Jerusalem music. The choirmaster examined it and nodded approval. "But come and hear us, to see if you think we will meet your needs." He led the way to the chapel, where the singers had assembled. The choir consisted of thirty-three voices divided into three registers. Monks with low voices and those of a medium vocal range were the majority and in about equal number. Three individuals represented the high register. Joshua wondered whether they were *falsetti* or *castrati*, as not one of them, in contrast to the other brothers, was bearded.

The singing started with an exercise. First, all three registers sounded simultaneously, then separately, and lastly the pitch levels met in an interlocking call-and-response escapade. It was quite a display although labeled just "scales." Four compositions followed. Three were chants—one plain, the next two-voiced, and the third multipolyphonic. Only the last piece of music had organ accompaniment by the choirmaster and sounded suspiciously Romantic. Musically there was no question but that the singing's quality was fit for a king—although Joshua was troubled by the three sopranos. He didn't want eunuchs, if that's what they were, at his coronation but decided to postpone asking. He and Sestius expressed their appreciation to the choirmaster, asked him to convey their thanks to the abbot, and left no doubt that they would soon be in touch about the coronation day schedule.

From the monastery to where biblical Jericho had been wasn't far, and with here-and-now Jericho being just a bit farther, they decided to explore. Joshua regretted not having a Baedeker along, but his was in cargo somewhere between Hoboken and Haifa. Among the three of them, though, and with the help of some weathered placards and signs, they were able to piece together an approximate advisory on the structures they were seeking and seeing. Past and prior pasts came and went here and became improbably intertwined. It was doubtful that the present could thrive, yet it was proving to be tenacious, persistent, fit to survive. Muslims, Christians, Jews, and all their subdivisions had a presence in Jericho as undoubtedly did some atheists, agnostics, and heathens. All claimed ownership of the sand, the stones, the little streams, and all, too, had dreams in which this land was their own.

The trio lingered longer than expected. The sun was setting as Benjamin turned the car toward Jerusalem. Suddenly its engine began to groan. Benjamin shut it off and let it cool, but when he started it up again it idled oddly. They decided to drive slowly to the closest habitation Benjamin knew of—the arts settlement—and indeed were able to arrive there without mishap. The place was a small oasis of palm trees and single-story houses surrounded by a wall and much emptiness. At the gate house, they were told that there was a resident mechanic, but she was away and wouldn't return until the middle of the next day. Sorry, in her absence, Benjamin would not be allowed into the repair shop. They would have to wait, which was no problem, though, since there was plenty of room in the guest quarters, and they could partake of the communal evening meal. Local rules would have to be followed while they were within the embrace of the settlement's walls—this was a nudist encampment, and they would be expected to disrobe. Joshua looked at Sestius. The monk had no visible reaction to the nudists' requirement.

Benjamin parked the car behind the gate house. They took their overnight bags out of the trunk and were pointed to the nearby guest quarters by the gatekeeper guard, who was fully dressed in military fatigues and also was well armed. "Shall we go and undress for dinner?" Joshua asked his companions. It was Benjamin, not Sestius, who betrayed discomfort.

They had separate rooms. Joshua undressed in his, went to the communal shower in which it turned out no one joined him, and returned to lie down on his bed and wait for the meal bell. It had been a long day, and he dozed off until the clanging woke him. He brushed and combed his hair, decided not to keep his sandals on, and went out into the hallway to meet his companions. Their doors were ajar, and he knocked on them. Benjamin was first to emerge. He had kept his socks and boots on, which added a bit of bulk to legs that were toothpick thin, balancing his mass of long locks and spread of chin hair. Not only was Benjamin scrawny between neck and ankles, but he wasn't even well hung. His was a modest, cut cock backed by a very small sack of a scrotum. The red of his pubic hair was like a flag calling attention to something that otherwise would have been overlooked.

Sestius kept them waiting a few moments, but when he stepped out into the hall, Joshua almost reeled back. A more resplendent specimen of male sexuality and ripe beauty would have been hard to imagine. This was manhood perfected, the musculature delineated, poised so that it gave the impression of straining at the bit and being ready to pounce yet holding perfectly still. The penis was so succulent it might have been about to erect itself, but instead Sestius's plush shaft obliged gravity by bouncing as if cushioned whenever he took a step forward. "What's the matter?" he asked Joshua who had blanched.

"Your tonsure is an affront to an ideal," he gulped. "You will be punished by all the gods on Olympus."

"I thought we promised not to heckle each other. Come, you two, let's find the dining hall." Sestius walked ahead, in the direction he thought right. Once outdoors, they could see others heading toward a long building that turned out to be not just for dining but the art colony's hall for meetings, parties, exhibits, and everything communal. Unlike the monastic dining hall they had visited earlier in the day, this one was full of noisy chatter. They, at least Joshua and Sestius, had expected Hebrew to be the predominant tongue, but it was English of various accents. The majority of the diners were women, thirty to fifty years old, and they insisted on splitting up the three male visitors and seating them at different tables. Sestius was escorted to the head table by a commanding female, who introduced herself as a sculptor and the colony's current presiding official. From where Joshua had been placed, he could see that she not only had given Sestius a place on the bench right next to herself but was all over him, touching his shoulder or arm every time she spoke to him and occasionally resting her hand on his thigh. This did not appear to fluster the monk in the slightest. Joshua wondered whether a male touch might have produced a spark or whether indeed Sestius was made of marble.

Benjamin hadn't really relaxed, but added to his initial discomfort about being undressed, there was now the stimulus of facing so many female breasts and triangles of pubic hair. He couldn't control himself; that mean little thing, his prick, became hard. He tried to cover the erection with a napkin, but, to the amusement of the ladies at his table, it formed a tiny yet noticeable tent on his lap. Benji's inexperience with the naked female body became quite apparent to everyone and prompted invitations to spend the night elsewhere than by himself in the guest quarters. After dinner, when everyone was gathered in the art gallery part of the building, it seemed as if Benjamin was about to accept one invitation when Sestius put a stop to it. "Nudity is one thing," he declared, "but fornication another. On this trip, Benjamin, you are working for the Roman Catholic Church and should behave in a suitable manner." Benjamin stood there chastened but with his erection still at full throttle. The three visitors bid goodnight to the colonists, who couldn't stop giggling. The trio returned to their rooms, but only Sestius fell asleep without further ado.

Breakfast the next morning was more sedate than dinner had been. Then the visitors explored the colony and a nearby grotto. When the mechanic returned from her trip shortly before noon, it turned out that just the addition of a can of lubricating oil calmed their car's engine.

Chapter Thirty Two

Yorkville Zara and Zurich Heinz

Joshua's schedule was stuffed like a holiday goose. No end of things needed to be sorted between the Haredim and Israel—agriculture, banking, defense, health, safety, taxation, transportation, zoning. Some issues seemed urgent, and Joshua was eager to work on the entire array, but both Aaron and Uri did not think anything would be settled soon. Taking time too were Joshua's visits to meet representative Haredim, Israelis, Palestinians, Druze, Maronites, Copts, Samaritans, Armenians, Assyrians, Circassians, Romani, assorted resident Africans, and Asians, plus the none-of-the-above present on biblical land. As with the diverse Habsburgs, he was a hit with the families. At one of the Palestinian homes, he found the kids up in a tree house they had built in their garden. Stopping the parents from calling them down, he instead climbed up to greet them on their turf. The tale of the tree-climbing Prince spread rapidly throughout the Palestinian communities and beyond. Also, Joshua asked Afsan to help him contact gay would-be activists. Whether they were of Jewish, Christian or Muslim families, the gays all operated underground. It just wasn't safe for them to be open. Miraculously those from different faiths did not object to mingling with each other at an initial meeting.

At the beginning of November, Zara Hoffmann finally telephoned. She and her human rights NGO group had arrived and were staying at a hotel in East Jerusalem. Zara took it as a given that Joshua would talk to her dozen about his plans as King of Jerusalem, but first she sought a quick private session for herself and one other he might be eager to see—Heinz Burckhardt. No, her husband wasn't along; she had left him back in New York.

It was the time of day when lights would be turning on in the neighborhoods of Jerusalem, those cupped into crevices of the lower-lying ground and those cradled closer to the sky on higher terrain and outcroppings. Colors were deeper than in the glare of full daylight. The atmosphere bathing the place was almost peaceful when Afsan ushered Zara and Heinz onto the roof garden of King House where Joshua and Aaron sat over documents. It was not unfitting for a designate king to be seen engaged in such a task against the panorama of the city shifting gear as the sun set and the first few stars began to shine. Joshua made quick introductions and was about to send Afsan off for drinks as Aaron gathered papers up and prepared to depart. Joshua suggested wine for this evening because, exploring local vintages, he was finding even the sharp sweetness of some to be intriguing. However, Zara rejected alcohol. She wanted to conform to the customs of the Mohammedan hosts of her group. Heinz remained silent and seemed oddly remote. He refrained from looking much at Joshua. It was both iced tea and wine that Afsan went to fetch as he accompanied Aaron downstairs.

Joshua felt that his guests were waiting for him to explain why he had dropped out of their lives so precipitously. Indeed, he'd not contacted the Hoffmanns since the night of the party Herby had hosted in New York, nor had he really tried while in Vienna to see Heinz in Zurich. "I was given a task when I got to Vienna, by a very persuasive individual, and find it has taken over my life. The demands are considerable. However, I think the work is worthwhile. At least and at last, I have a cause beyond myself to believe in."

"The only worthwhile cause here is to give Palestine, all of it, to the Palestinians and put an end to Zionism. That should be your task," Zara retorted. "And if you can use the ultra-orthodox Jews as a wedge against Zionism and as a lever to topple the Israeli Jews, all the more power to you."

"Zara, you have just arrived, haven't yet seen a thing, and already are unpacking your prejudices. There are others besides Jews and so-called Palestinians who want title to this land and have some sort of legitimate claim. For instance, the Samaritans. They are as ancient as any of the factions and have been dealt with badly by all the others."

"'As ancient,' "you say. "Yes, they are antiques, curiosities. Numerically they are negligible. They don't add up to much."

"Since when do mere numbers determine what is just? Once there were many, over a million, Samaritans. Just because they have been the victims of genocides, you deny them their homeland rights?"

"Culturally, too, they are insignificant, inferior. What have Samaritans contributed to civilization? Not even the cuckoo clock."

"Zara, you talk like a Nazi pig. How can you hold such disgusting views?"

Heinz's face had begun flushing. He couldn't contain himself any longer. "Joshua, you've changed. You used to be a gentleman. Now you argue like a shyster. Stop insulting Zara. The Jew in you has come out, and he is ugly. Your nose looks more hooked. Have you had yourself circumcised? It is you who have become an abomination."

"There is no shortage of hatreds in this barren land. What you two bring will barely be noticeable. Instead of my rude, crude new self, I'll send the Vatican's representative, Brother Sestius, to lecture to your group," Joshua replied in a weary voice.

What Joshua had heard from Zara and Heinz seemed to him so trivial, so petty, so beside the point that he couldn't even muster much anger. Afsan had returned carrying a tray with an open bottle of chilled white wine, a closed bottle of chilled soda water, a small pitcher of iced tea, glasses, and napkins.

Joshua picked up the wine bottle and looked at its label. "Ah, we have here some Samaritan wine. May I pour you some, Heinz?" However, Zara and Heinz had gotten up from their chairs, nodded to each other, and were departing without a word of goodbye. Afsan was obliged to conduct them downstairs and let them out. After they had gone, Joshua poured himself a glass of the vintage from which a whiff of citron reached his nostrils. He took two sips that gave him a stronger sense of citrus but also left the slight aftertaste of cinnamon, so he opened the soda water to pour himself a chaser. Alone on the roof, he toasted a bright planet that had emerged in the sky. It struck him that it might be Mercury.

Chapter Thirty Three

Telephoning

Tasks had really taken over Joshua's life in Jerusalem. Not just visits to acquaint him with the place and its people plus the planning sessions to begin adjusting Haredi relations with all others, but looming too on his schedule were language lessons, vocabulary study times, periods to practice pronunciation. As a linguistics major and then translator, Joshua had learned Hebrew. For the first time, though, he now had the chance to actually use it. He also wanted to understand the local Arabic and, ultimately, to know Aramaic plus the Samaritan tongues that were cousins to Hebrew and Arabic. Indeed, Joshua had changed; Heinz was right in that there was a distinct difference between Joshua now, the new Joshua and the young man he had been in New York. What that change was, though, Heinz hadn't discerned. No longer was Joshua self centered. He didn't worry about himself anymore; there was no fretting to optimize all waking moments; he wasn't perpetually under pressure from himself about having to decide. He no longer felt obliged to enjoy. Joshua had chosen when taking on the Jerusalem assignment and didn't anymore consider himself an end, a goal, an individual with inalienable rights. The current Joshua saw himself as a means, a tool, an instrument.

It was another instrument—the telephone—that brought home the extent of the transformation. Suddenly, the long distance line that had been installed in King House began to hum and Joshua realized that he had been neglecting not just Zara and Heinz but also the Countess Zdenka, His Highness, Herby, Josef Heine. A steady stream of calls was triggered by Frl. Andrea ringing first from Germany, next from Brussels, then from somewhere else that the needs of United Europe had taken His Highness. She reminded Joshua that he should, ought, must keep His Highness informed of how matters were getting on with the Haredim and how plans for the coronation were firming up. Brother Sestius had been sending written reports to the Vatican and presumably identical copies to His Highness, but His Highness strongly felt these were no substitute for regular telephone contact between himself and his nephew. On hearing that, Joshua resolved to also keep the countess informed. The weekly or more frequent conversations he initiated with her concerned events less than they did his inner life, how calm his responses had become and what seemed to him the new selflessness of his moods.

Joshua described his break with Zara and Heinz and how matter-of-factly, how painlessly for him it had happened.

"Don't for an instant believe that you no longer possess an ego," the countess advised him. "It is just that the objective goal, the impersonal role you have adopted makes you less vulnerable. You tell yourself it isn't you, the inner being, the intimate self who has been forgetful of old friends. It is the designate king, the player of a part who has had to behave so."

A phone call also came from Josef Heine to tell Joshua that the bank restitution had come through. Joshua was now a rich man. "The first thing you ought to do is to make a will. If an ordinary estate is left in limbo by the death of its owner, no big problem. Wealth, though, ought to belong or it will cause woes, wars, and worse. Give me instructions as to who will be your heir or heirs."

Joshua hadn't before owned anything worthy of making a will about. Of the people he cared for, it was probably the countess who would need funds, and he intended to leave her some. Perhaps, too, Ruth in Salonika. Would eventually Afsan require a stipend? Their wants, though, were modest. Ought he to subsidize a cause? That would take careful thought. Right now Joshua had too much else to consider.

How to contact Herby, Joshua had no idea. Herby might be anywhere. The superstitious thought kept recurring to Joshua that if he wished hard enough and Herby really were needed, he would turn up. Herby was certainly one guest he wanted at the coronation, along with the countess, Ruth, Frl. Andrea. Any of the New Yorkers he had known? First things first though: the King of Jerusalem project had still, luckily, not been picked up by the press. Undoubtedly, that was due to His Highness's keeping himself remote until it was time to announce the coronation, and, so far, Joshua was still gathering information, getting acquainted, and hadn't yet made a statement. Perhaps it was time for him to call a conference, give an audience, and take a stand.

Chapter Thirty Four

Stakeholders

One morning, Aaron voiced dissatisfaction with Joshua's busy schedule. "There isn't time enough for all you want to do," he complained, as he and Joshua were considering the week ahead. "So much of it too, now, doesn't deal directly with Haredi business. Some of my rabbi colleagues are complaining about that. From the vantage of Israel, too, I've heard Uri say that your concern with the minorities—the Samaritans, the Arameics, the Druse, and so forth—is bothersome. You were invited to administer Haredim-Israeli relations but not to stir up hornets' nests."

"As the King of Jerusalem, all of its people are and should be of concern to me. Nowhere in the history of that title have I seen its rule limited to just one of the populations here. I think it is time to hold a stakeholder's meeting and establish my domain."

"Before the coronation? You have been able to escape scrutiny so far. As your secretary, I can testify how hard you work on Haredi issues. I could also testify about your grander ambitions. I support them but am certain many of my people do not. For them, the rights of others are simply more excuses to deny justice to us, the founders of Jerusalem."

"Publicity will come of its own accord. My announcing my policy now to all the factions will save us time. Individual, one-on-one sessions with each camp will undoubtedly have to follow. Yes, Aaron, let's call the stakeholders together in a week's time!"

The guest list to attend the designate King of Jerusalem's introduction was kept to a minimum. Would the great ground-floor room of King House be able to accommodate all? Only by limiting each of Jerusalem's ethnic or religious entities to three attendees and each international or national stakeholder to just two. Press access couldn't be limited without prompting complaints about restricting freedom to the news. Invitations were issued hastily by the UN's Jerusalem Office. As it turned out, there were more local entities than had been anticipated but fewer international and national stakeholders asked to come. The only reporter who definitely bit on accepting was Pamela from the alternative New York weekly *The Village Voice*. She had been at Herby's party for Joshua in New York. With her, the name Joshua Haburghe, given in the invitation, had rung three bells. Pamela was a dance fan and had read Haburghe's reports in *Ballet Review*. She also, as a hobby, kept up on Europe's noble houses and had heard the rumor about another Habsburg male being recognized by the official lineage. And she kept up with reparations for what the Nazis had done and noted the settlement of the Heine Bank case. Joshua Habsburg Heine, alias Josh Haburghe, had peeked Pamela's curiosity, and she had persuaded her editors to send her to Jerusalem.

Chapter Thirty Five

A Time to Put Toys Aside

The number of people invited to the stakeholders' meeting and who they were prompted Israel to station security forces at points of access to King House. It had taken UN pressure to obtain safe passage for certain Palestinians. At the last moment, additional press applied to attend. Joshua wanted no other speakers, no one to introduce him, no questions immediately following his talk. If particular stakeholders demanded answers or wished to be querulous, separate sessions to give satisfaction or for venting would be scheduled between this meeting and the coronation. The sole hurdle the planners foresaw in preparing the stakeholders' meeting was the quantity of ice needed to serve iced tea to everyone.

Joshua had decided not to make an entrance but to be in the Great Room from the start, from 9:30 a.m. when, according to the official announcement, the doors to King House would be opened. As an American, he had opted for the casual formality of an on-the-range dress code—some cowboy paraphernalia, such as a white shirt with large cuffs and collar, a bola at the neck, a dark vest, good blue jeans, boots. Luckily, the one outfit of this sort he owned was not in the crates on its way to Haifa but still in his New York apartment and could be air-expressed to Jerusalem.

Also present jointly from the beginning of the meeting were Aaron in his rabbinical garb, Brother Sestius in his cassock, the head of the UN's Israel Mission in his business attire. Benjamin had been engaged to help at the gate of King House, and Afsan, with two of the part-time women, served the iced tea as arrivals stepped in to the Great Room.

Uri, in business suit but without a necktie and the USA ambassador, who was cuff linked and tie clipped, arrived just after 9:30 a.m. Joshua went up to those entering, greeted them, and introduced himself when necessary. People tended not to take seats right away and, if not conversing with those representing other entities, at least nodded hello and sometimes toasted each other by raising the frosty glasses of tea and taking a sip. The room filled, and as the 10 a.m. hour was about to strike, Joshua stepped up onto the dais at the far end of the space. It had a tall chair, a small table, a microphone, a hand bell. He rang the bell, asked everyone to be seated, seated himself, and moved the microphone close.

"Good morning. Most of you I've met already, but just in case not, I am Joshua Habsburg Heine and have been invited to be in Jerusalem by the United Nations at the suggestions of this city's residents known as the Haredim—adherents of an ancient and strict form of the Judaic religion. The Haredim feel the practical need for a temporal administration. For religious reasons they cannot accept mundane rule by their own rabbinate, nor can they recognize the state of Israel. Only when the Messiah comes can there be governance by someone who is a Jew. Until then, they consider any Jew designated to rule a false Messiah. It so happens that an old title, King of Jerusalem, persists from the days of the Crusades. The Haredim have petitioned the United Nations to reaffirm the title's validity and to install its current holder as their governor in temporal matters. In religious matters, they will continue to be guided by the deliberations of their rabbinate.

History does not happen quite like a species' natural evolution. It is concocted of necessity, accident, whimsy. Most of us will have learned about the existence of the King of Jerusalem title only recently. I think I'm not alone in having been astonished to realize that it persists still and possesses a certain validity in international law. It proved useful at the time of the Crusades, was recognized by the Vatican and other Christian churches as well as by the Moslem Caliphates and came to be acknowledged by the Haredi Jews. Apparently, the United Nations Organization has no problem with it either. Inheritance of the title has for many generations now been within the Habsburg family, sometimes designated as the Habsburg-Lorraine lineage or the House of Austria. The current bearer of that title is Otto von Habsburg, also known as Dr. Otto Habsburg. He was the last crown prince of the Empire of Austria-Hungary. He is at this time president of the International Paneuropean Union, an office to which he is devoting all of his time. He has designated me, a fraternal nephew, to fulfill his obligations as King of Jerusalem, and I have agreed to carry out that work. I consider it an honor to be chosen. The title will be passed to me by my uncle in a coronation ceremony before the end of this year, to be precise on December 10. Today, I want to tell you how I see the King of Jerusalem functioning at this time, in 1977. Undoubtedly, my explanation will leave you with questions, with objections, with suggestions. You will have time to formulate your thoughts between now and December 10. Separate discussion sessions will be set up at the request of each stakeholder entity. Please contact the Rabbi Aaron ben Ai, my secretary, to schedule your appointment."

Joshua paused to taste the iced tea. Having done so, he signaled for a wedge of lemon, and while Afsan brought it to his table and squeezed it into his glass, Joshua looked around the room. Expressions were noncommittal or bemused yet attentive. He could continue.

"What is the job description I see for the King of Jerusalem? Both terms, "King" and "Jerusalem," need to be defined. Kings today are not absolute monarchs. As mentioned already, I will hold no religious sway over the Haredi Jews and their habitations. The job will be that of administrator in temporal matters. Can one, though, separate the temporal from the eternal? Transportation is just one example of how religion and the mundane are intertwined. Religion commands the Haredim not to permit vehicular traffic on the Sabbath. Closing streets to cars from sunset Friday to sunset Saturday was easy to do as long as the Haredim lived in well-defined neighborhoods. That, however, is beginning to be no longer the case. All populations are outgrowing their traditional hives. Those who celebrate either the Friday, the Saturday, or the Sunday as Sabbath are having to share doorsteps, not to mention that there are different ways of defining a day—is it sunset to sunset or midnight to midnight? For the King of Jerusalem to assure the Haredim of the sanctity of the Sabbath and not have every other citizen of Jerusalem forced to a standstill will be tricky. I trust that the most resourceful of Jerusalem's rabbis, the most jurisprudent of the city's Jesuits, the most incisive of its imams will make themselves available to consult on this and similar predicaments."

Joshua could see worry gathering on the brows of Aaron, present as his secretary, and the two official Haredi representatives. Others in the room wore let's-wait-and-see expressions.

"Historically the King of Jerusalem ruled not just over the most obser- vant Jews, or unobservant Jews, or Christians, or Moslems. He admin- istered for everyone—including the Druse, Samaritans, Aramaeans, et al. For that sweeping jurisdiction not to continue, the title and tradition would have to be changed." Much buzz followed this statement. Joshua thought he heard a loud whisper—the phrase "a power grab" tickled in his ears. He ignored it and it subsided, so he went on.

"Finally, I want to clarify the boundaries of the city. Jerusalem was not just an urban nucleus at the time of the first Crusader king but con- tained much open land. It was a veritable province. Its extent included Mediterranean sand beaches to the west of the city, the Jordan River's val- leys and adjacent peaks to the immediate east, also stretches of unplanted plateau into the desert beyond. It is land claimed and disputed by Jews, Arabs, others. Arguments to prove and counter these claims have been made based on the Bible and other traditions, based on archeology, and recently on chemistry—the consistency of people's, families', tribes', nations' genes. None of this evidence has proven that any single group owned a particular parcel of land. Not even the Canaanites were here first or exclusively. The only sensible, the sole just solution is to recognize all claimants to the territory and within it establish not a one-state or a two- state solution but a no-state solution, to divorce nationality from territory. The land should be owned by all, that is by the United Nations. On that land, an Israeli citizen can live as an Israeli citizen under a different government than his next-door Palestinian neighbor whose allegiance is to a Palestinian government. The same for the Druse, Samaritans, Aramaeans and all others. Towns and townships, neighborhoods, enclaves, settlements, homesteads and houses, apartments, and even rooms-for-rent may be leased with UN approval to individuals or groups of this or that nationality."

Joshua wasn't finished and continued with "Citizenship, like religion, will finally be divorced from land, from territory, from borders. How can this not be an advance for humanity? It is a way the world as a whole is tending. Just consider how many dual citizenships, even triples, exist already, and doesn't that invalidate the old concept of country? The Province of Jerusalem as home for no single nation but for all will just be ahead of the rest of the world in this important respect."

He had still more to say, "The idea may be odd, but it is not absurd. Just consider the alternatives. A one-state, two-nations country has been proposed, a Palestisrael. So have two states, Israel and Palestine. The first will institutionalize immense inequities between the two major populations. Which will out produce the other, which will outbreed the other? Ignored will be the rights of all the non-Palestinians, non-Israelis, the "minority" citizens. The second will spawn endless disputes about borders, will instigate perpetual wars. Also it avoids the question of whether there isn't already a Palestinian state called Jordan. The only sensible, civilized solution to current quandaries is the no-state proposal. I thank you for your attention."

There was dead silence. No applause. No rustling, no chair squeaking. Not an iota of noise could be discerned. People were not sure they had heard correctly and waited as if frozen. Finally, one delegate went up to Aaron and asked whether a printed version of the remarks was available. Aaron consulted with Joshua briefly and announced that a photocopy would be delivered to everyone on the guest list. People departed in a dour mood.

Chapter Thirty Six

Post Mortem

The print-out promised the stakeholders was quickly produced. Benjamin, Afsan, and additional messengers distributed it later that day and into the night. Responses were received at King House even before the next morning. Wondering whether this Joshua Habsburg Heine was simple minded, was mad, was a jokester were Israel, practically all Palestinian entities, Jordan, and partisan groups like the World Zionist Federation and the neo-Nazis of Zara Hoffmann's Parity for Palestine. There was no way the Israelis, Palestinians, Jordanians would abstain from ruling land. Without territory, they saw themselves losing power and prestige. Jordan, having been declared Palestinian by Joshua, actually withdrew its representatives for several hours, until reminded that it had once subscribed to dreams about a United Arab Republic—a union undone by the prospect of it having just one vote in the UN whereas the separate Arab states commanded a cluster.

Most of the semi-stakeholders, the observers—countries like the USA and the UK, and the more impartial NGOs like the Red Cross, were puzzled, perplexed, and had resorted to scratching their heads. Only the minority stakeholders liked the no-state solution, but of course these Aramaeans, Druse, Samaritans, et al. counted for nothing. The sole strong supporter of the idea of a no-state solution was the UN's bureaucracy. The dissolution of borders they wanted ultimately for the world could begin here and now. His Highness had been faxed Joshua's statement ahead of time. Being an internationalist, he had responded enthusiastically.

It was the Vatican's Brother Sestius in consultation with the UN staff who saved Joshua's idea and the prospect of his coronation. Israel, Jordan, and a presumed Palestine would not be abolished in the fore- seeable future. Implementation of the no-state solution would happen in stages. Each stage would be of long, very long, duration and would depend on the success of each immediately preceding arrangement. Initially, the King of Jerusalem would rule those originally envisioned—the Haredim— and in addition just the small number of people who belonged to other religious or ethnic minorities. The term Jerusalem would be somewhat more broadly defined to include Haredi Jews and other minorities outside the strict city limits of Jerusalem, but the king would have no jurisdiction over Israeli Jews and Christians or any Jordanians wherever they lived.

Refinement of and agreement on this compromise would be dis- cussed at a second general meeting to be organized not by the designate King of Jerusalem but by the UN. Leading up to it were the individual ses- sions Joshua had promised the stakeholders and observers.

There were lots of these little sessions. Haggling became the order of the day. Every few hours, a different delegation called on King House to make proposals. While several UN staffers, Sestius, and Aaron tried to appease those angered and plodded away at compromise, Joshua was showing signs of impatience.

For a while, Joshua let himself be distracted by the interviews the *Village Voice* reporter Pamela was conducting with him. She was a person who doted on preparation. Gathering data was her favorite part of being a reporter. She'd go on and on until her editor ordered her to stop sleuth- ing and start summing up. In conversation with Joshua, she was pains- taking in repeatedly asking the same questions in different disguises. Pamela didn't seem like an inquisitor, though. That would have turned Joshua off. He thought of her as a plodder who wanted to get things right. Also, Pamela showed more interest in Joshua's pre-Jerusalem life than he himself could currently muster. That amused him. She managed to hold his attention for much of three days, and when he put a stop to her interviews, she didn't become upset. Moving on instead to his contacts,

Pamela questioned those present in Jerusalem in person and telephoned those who were in Europe and New York. With them also, she seemed not like a snooper but a pedantic perfectionist.

When Joshua declared Pamela's sessions with him over, the haggling with the stakeholders was still going on. He realized he needed to escape, that he had to be by himself, so he announced that he was taking a trip. For some time, he had wished to see Sodom, wanted to know what the lowest spot on the face of the earth felt like. He asked Benjamin to drive him there. Sestius objected. Joshua was needed at the second conference. Why not, though, hold it at Sodom? There was a salt spa at the location. It could be leased and secured. Moreover, the remoteness of the place would simplify safety arrangements and cut down on the number of attendees. The fewer the better. Were everyone who had attended the stakeholders' meeting at King House to travel to Sodom, discussions would be everlasting.

Salt, not sand, rims the Dead Sea's shoreline. Grains of it sparkle in the sun. Columns of salt, like the ghosts of Lot's wife and daughters, undulated in a heat higher than Joshua had ever felt before. The air above pressed down, its weight oppressing human sense. The waters of the Dead Sea were slippery and burned the skin. How easy it could be to lose one's mind at the lowest spot on the face of the earth. No one lived here permanently.

Those who worked at mining minerals in this white, gray, yellow landscape resided on higher ground and were transported in and out. Joshua wondered whether it had been a mistake to stay and plan a meeting at this place. Some of the delegates weren't youngsters. Would people adjust to this pressure chamber?

Unexpected was the appearance of Pamela's article about Joshua on the day before the Sodom conference. Although few people in Jerusalem had direct access to her publication, the contents of the piece were sensational enough that they were summarized the next morning by daily papers and newscasts throughout the Near East. Pamela's portrait of Joshua seemed benign on the surface, yet it highlighted his every feature a partisan of this part of the world could consider a blemish. From conversation with Heinz, Pamela had confirmed the fact that Joshua's maternal family was Jewish. That would make him ineligible to rule the Haredim in their eyes. That he was heir to a Heine banking fortune made him unsympathetic to Israeli and Palestinian leftist parties. That he claimed to be an atheist made him objectionable to the religious, as did Pamela's insinuation that he was gay. Comparatively, Joshua's other traits which were mentioned—his diplomatic skills, language facility, peace proposal, and sense of justice, hard work, personal charm—appeared trivial.

Chapter Thirty Seven

Salt

Joshua rose early on the morning of the Sodom conference. From a newscast he listened to while brushing his teeth, gargling, shaving, showering, dressing, combing his hair, he learned that Pamela's article had appeared and surmised what it had revealed. The best thing for him now would be to ignore it, not read it yet and be able to enter the conference as if nothing were amiss. There was at some distance from the resort a geological formation that he wanted to see close up. It would be too hot to walk there later in the day, and there was time enough before the conference session began.

He set off by himself before breakfast. In the early morning light, the sulfur deposit in the salt strata turned this entire wasteland to gold. On the path he was following, he sometimes lost sight of his destination. There were bluffs in the way that looked like the weathered walls of fortifications. An immense silence lay on the land, broken only by the crunch of his steps on the ground. Suddenly, he heard a sharp crack, a small explosion at some distance. He was about to stop walking and listen for more when he felt a singe pass through his chest. Nothing else occurred instantly, but then an immense pain flared up in his torso, and Joshua fell. He must have been lying on the path for some minutes when awareness returned. Raising himself on his elbows, he still perceived the pain—intense as an inferno yet somehow at a distance. He tried to keep it away. The space between himself and the hurt held; he could think. Someone was coming toward him on the path. He was sure it was help arriving. Good, because he knew he was losing blood rapidly. Bending over him was Herby, as welcoming and as wonderful looking as the day they had met, last summer at the beach when he had seemed to be a Hermes figure born from the surf. Hermes knelt beside Joshua, then sat down next to him, raised his shoulders, turned him over to see where he was bleeding. With clear eyes and a sigh, Hermes placed Joshua's head on his lap so that they could look at each other.

"You are dying, Joshua, and there's nothing that can be done about it. I do not have the power to undo human deeds. Do you want to know who shot you? No. And it doesn't matter, there were quite a few who wanted to. Why spoil your last moments thinking about them. If your eyes can still focus and form a clear image, look deep into the sky and at this crust of earth. Under these heavens and near this spot legendary things have happened. You too can become historic, a hero, immortal. As Hermes, that power I do have. I can call witnesses to this place. Your body will be found, the crime investigated, Pamela will write the full story and become your Homer. Children to come will read about you trying to bring justice and peace to Jerusalem. Do you want that?"

"You gods can be tempted, I know. Let us bargain. I'll swap the status, the fame, the immortality you offer for a more soothing reward. Perhaps you'll think it petty, practical. I am dying without having made a will. Swear you will see to it that my money will sustain three people who have cared for me and who may come to need support."

"Gods cannot swear, unless you think we too have gods, but most of us are atheists. I will see to it that part of your Heine Bank inheritance amply sustains the Countess Zdenka, Ruth, and Afsan. Trusts for them, though, will require only a small part of that fortune. What should happen with the bulk of it? Hadn't you a foundation in mind?"

"People are limited, they die, but while they live are definite. The purposes for which foundations are set up may have infinite scope, may be noble and unending, but they can become worthlessly vague. It would be nice to terminate nationalism and territoriality and to battle religious suicide and celibacy with my money but how to eliminate those who uphold those concepts—the heads of state, the pope, the Dalai Lama, even the secretary general of the UN who recognizes states rather than individuals. Shoot them, like me? No. If there is to be a foundation, let people and not an abstract purpose set its path. The people I'd trust are three of my cousins— the painter-banker Josef Heine and on the Habsburg side the astronomer Christina and the nun Gertrude. Pauses between Joshua's words were growing longer. "Herby, how you shine ..." was said in a whisper.

It was custom in the first books of the Bible, in the old texts written in Samaritan, to bury the dead where they had last prayed. Hermes, following the ancient prescription, used his bare hands to dig Joshua's grave. He lowered the body into the ground, where it lay curled, like napping in bed after having enjoyed love. Soon handfuls of grains, pebbles, and small round rocks of Sodom salt from the surroundings covered it completely.

www.ingramcontent.com/pod-product-compliance
Lightning Source LLC
Chambersburg PA
CBHW060230180626
46813CB00007B/3022